"Why don't we wait until morning to explore the grounds?"

Guy suggested.

Lia shook her head. "It's still light enough to see. Besides, don't the experts say snakes try to avoid humans?"

"I'm no expert, but it sounds reasonable. We're a dangerous species. Killers, one and all."

She slanted him a look. "Speak for yourself."

"It's true. All human beings are capable of killing if the right occasion arises. Fortunately for the survival of the species, most of us would only kill to save ourselves or someone we love, but the potential's there, all the same."

Lia looked at her new acquaintance and wondered what he was actually trying to say....

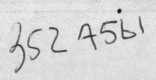

Dear Reader,

We've got another month of eerily romantic reading for you, with another of your favorite authors contributing an irresistible book to the line.

The Woman in White is by veteran writer Jane Toombs. An exploration of her family history leads Lia Courtois to Guy Russell, whose past seems inextricably entwined with hers. Their futures, too, seem to be heading down a shared pathway—but only if they can escape the woman in white, whose deadly influence may deprive them of any future at all.

As always, I hope you'll enjoy your journey to the dark side of love, and that you'll come back next month for *Something Beautiful*, by Marilyn Tracy.

Yours,

Leslie Wainger
Senior Editor and Editorial Coordinator

Please address questions and book requests to:
Silhouette Reader Service
U.S.: 3010 Walden Ave., P.O. Box 1325, Buffalo, NY 14269
Canadian: P.O. Box 609, Fort Erie, Ont. L2A 5X3

JANE TOOMBS

The Woman in White

Published by Silhouette Books
America's Publisher of Contemporary Romance

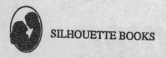 SILHOUETTE BOOKS

ISBN 0-373-27050-X

THE WOMAN IN WHITE

Books by Jane Toombs

Silhouette Shadows

JANE TOOMBS

believes that a touch of the mysterious adds spice to a romance. Her childhood fascination with stories about shape changers such as vampires, werewolves and shamans never faded, leading to her present interest in surpernatural influences, not only in Gothic romances but in the early cultures of all peoples.

A Californian transplanted to New York, Jane lives in the shadow of Storm King Mountain.

PROLOGUE

Five-year-old Guy Russell whimpered and turned over in his sleep. Outside the house the moon broke through the clouds and sent a shaft of light through his bedroom window, light as pale and ethereal as the woman who wove through his dream.

"Zha," she whispered to him. *"Zha ray ve en."*

He knew she was a woman and that she was beautiful, even though he couldn't see her very well. She was misty, like the fog off the ocean. And, though he couldn't understand what she said, he knew she wanted him to go with her.

He felt a yearning to go with her but he was scared—not of the pale woman so much as of the darkness he feared she meant to lead him into. It wasn't the regular kind of dark, like at night in California. Her darkness was somewhere else, it was the kind of dark that would swallow him up so he'd be lost forever and ever.

She raised her white hand and motioned to him to come to her. He tried to say no, but he couldn't speak. He tried to run away from her, but he couldn't move. And all the time she drifted closer and closer. So close he could finally see her face clearly. Her smile both beckoned and repelled him. He feared if she ever touched him something bad would happen. Something awful bad. But frightened as he was, part of him wanted her to touch him. And that scared him even more.

Helpless, unable to move, he watched her misty hands come closer and closer, reaching for him. He sobbed in terrified anticipation....

Something touched him. He screamed. His eyes flew open, and he stared uncomprehendingly into his mother's worried face.

"It's all right, sweetheart," his mother crooned, gathering him into her arms. "You're safe with me, nothing can hurt you."

Held close to her sweet-smelling softness, his fear slowly ebbed and he began to relax. His eyes drooped closed. Just before sleep overtook him, he heard his father's voice, deep and low.

"Is Guy all right?"

"He was moaning," his mother said, "so I came in to check on him. He was having one of his bad dreams."

"Again?" his father asked. "Is that normal?"

She sighed. "Sometimes I wonder if his dreams come from—well, from before."

"Before what?" his father asked. "Newborn babies don't have any past. No befores."

Because Guy didn't quite understand what his father meant about babies not having befores, the words stuck in his mind, temporarily halting his drift toward sleep.

"I know I'm being foolish," his mother said. "The doctor told me children usually grow out of these dreams and not to worry about Guy because he's a healthy, normal child."

"I'm sure the doctor's right." Father used his nononsense voice.

"Yes, of course. And I do believe him. There's nothing wrong with Guy, nothing at all. He's our perfect little boy. We're so fortunate to have him and we'll never, ever let anything hurt him."

Guy slipped into sleep, comforted, believing that his mother was always right.

He couldn't know how wrong she was....

CHAPTER ONE

Impatiently waiting for his last client of the day to arrive, Guy Russell paced restlessly about the law office that had once been his father's and now was his. He paused to gaze from one of the corner windows at the wedding cake cupola atop Oakland's city hall and found himself reminded of the pleasure his father, a history buff, had taken in telling clients that President Taft himself had laid the cornerstone for the building back in 1911.

The memory brought him no pleasure. He disliked remembering anything about his father these days, even though he'd loved and trusted him. Once.

Not now. Even his mother's memory was tarnished beyond recall. Why had they lied to him?

Why hadn't they ever told him he'd been adopted? Guy hadn't discovered the truth until after his father's death, when he went through his private files and found not only the adoption papers but a gold locket containing a woman's picture. His methodical father had tagged the locket as "Jane Doe's." Since his mother had died five years ago, there was nobody left to confront except his uncles, the two other attorneys in the firm of Russell, Russell and Russell.

All he'd learned was that, while both Uncle Tim and Uncle Howard had known about the adoption, they'd never been given any details. Uncle Howard, however, did manage to remember hearing about Guy's birth mother coming to Oakland from New Orleans and dying a few days after he was born.

"You know your mother worked as a volunteer at the county hospital," Uncle Howard had added. "I suspect she learned enough about the woman to decide then and there that you were the baby she'd always wanted. But that's conjecture. Your mother kept her secrets and your father always played his cards close to his vest. I don't know anything more."

Guy's own investigation had uncovered his original birth certificate but, with the mother listed as Jane Doe and no address and the father listed as Unknown, it had proved a dead end.

Perhaps it was ridiculous, as Uncle Tim had insisted, for a thirty-two-year-old man to feel betrayed by his dead parents, but Guy couldn't help it. Neither of his uncles sympathized with his driving urge to uncover his true parentage. "Best to let sleeping dogs lie," was Uncle Tim's advice.

Guy still thought he'd find answers in New Orleans while they were both certain his upcoming trip to that city would be a waste of time and effort.

Guy glanced at his watch. His client was five minutes late—he would give her another five minutes, no more. His plane was leaving in two hours and he damn well didn't intend to miss it. Technically this woman wasn't really his client, anyway. She'd been referred to him by Uncle Tim because Guy specialized in wills and inheritances.

How could he explain to anyone, let alone his never-had-an-irrational-thought uncles, that it was almost as though he were being summoned to New Orleans? As though genetic cords were inexorably drawing him back to where his mother had come from. And, quite likely, his father as well. The feeling grew stronger every day that he *must* go.

His intercom buzzed, alerting him that the client had arrived. Since he'd already told Sadie to send her in at once, he waited for the door to open, hoping the woman wouldn't turn out to be a long-winded type with a million questions.

The door eased open and a dark-haired young woman hesitated on the threshold as though wondering if she should enter or not. Guy walked toward her, prepared to usher her in without any more delay. She tossed her hair back from her face and stared at him. When his gaze met hers, he stopped abruptly, temporarily speechless.

She was tall for a woman, with eyes as brown as dark chocolate dominating an appealing ivory pale face framed by a mass of wavy black hair. She wore a simple navy blue suit with a white blouse. She was beautiful—but her beauty wasn't what affected him so strongly.

He knew her, he was positive he knew her, and yet at the same time he was equally certain they'd never met.

Trying to dispel the strange sensation gripping him, he reached out and took her arm to guide her inside. As he touched her, the room seemed to shimmer around him, then it disappeared and he was standing with this woman under a full-moon whose silver light glinted off dark water. She held out her arms to him and he reached for her....

Guy blinked in confusion and found himself back in his office. What the hell was the matter with him? The woman shook off his hand, her dark eyes troubled. Realizing she was poised to flee—and how could he blame her?—he managed to pull himself together.

"I'm Guy Russell," he told her, taking a step back as he tried for formality, hoping his attorney-client manner would reassure her. "And you must be Ms.—" He searched his mind for her name and found it. Thank God his wits hadn't entirely deserted him. "—Ms. Courtois. Please come in and sit down."

For a moment he thought she would refuse, then she took a deep breath and walked into the room. Nodding toward the chair next to his desk, he shut the door.

Perched uneasily on the edge of the chair, Lia Courtois watched the tall, auburn-haired man walk around the desk and sit behind it. As she tried to avoid looking into his eyes—the predatory, golden eyes of a leopard—a nagging sense of familiarity hovered just beyond the edge of reason.

When he'd taken her hand, she'd been positive that somewhere, sometime, he'd touched her before—and not just her hand. She tingled with the certainty that this meeting would be dangerous for them both.

Impossible! He was a complete, utter stranger. She must have reacted to the strong chemistry between them, a chemistry she could feel flowing now, an intense, disturbing current of awareness. And, despite his attempt to be all business, she knew he felt the same electric thrill she did.

Lia sat up straight. Man-woman chemistry was something determination could overcome. She'd suffered from overreacting to it once in her life—but never again.

"Ms. Courtois," he said, "I believe you're here to consult me about a legacy."

His voice was deep and smooth, a voice she doubted she'd ever tire of listening to. Lia pushed the notion firmly aside and cleared her throat.

"Several days ago I received a letter from a New Orleans law firm," she said, noticing as she pulled an envelope from her bag that he'd leaned forward, his gaze intent, as though she'd said something of great interest. Telling herself it was merely his professional manner, she offered him the envelope, saying, "I believe it will save time if you read the letter before I continue."

What a shock that letter had been. She felt as though her entire world had been turned upside down.

She tried and failed to keep her mind on why she was here rather than on the man she was consulting. He looked to be no more than a few years older than her own twenty-seven years and there was no question about his attractiveness. His longish auburn hair, curling at his collar, and those unusual leopard eyes, combined with a solid, rangy build, made him knock-'em-dead gorgeous.

Lia frowned, giving herself a mental shake. She was here on a legal matter, not to evaluate the man's charms. She could trust him to explain the ins and outs of the law but not otherwise. Men like Guy, who carried charisma with them like an invisible aura, were definitely not to be trusted when it came to personal involvement.

Guy put the letter down and looked at her. "As far as I can tell this appears to be the straightforward announcement of an inheritance—if you're the Ophelia Vangel Courtois mentioned here."

"Lia," she corrected involuntarily. "I mean, yes, that's the name on my birth certificate, but I've never gone by Ophelia. At first I didn't see how they could mean me, but..." She paused and shook her head, tension coiling inside her. "It seems they do."

"You have some doubts?"

"I never knew I had a great-aunt, much less one named Marie-Louise de la Roche!" The words burst from her. "I never knew I had *any* relatives except my

grandparents, who raised me. They—they lied to me.''
Her voice broke and tears gathered in her eyes.

Knowing exactly how she felt, Guy's heart went out
to her. With difficulty he conquered his impulse to
leap from his chair and pull her into his arms to comfort her. Hugging any client was out of bounds. Hugging this one would be a disaster.

"It's devastating to realize those we love have de-
ceived us," he told her.

Evidently recognizing the sincerity in his voice she
stopped dabbing at her eyes with a tissue and gave him
a searching look.

To his surprise, Guy found himself sharing his own
problem with her. "I know, because it happened to
me. I didn't discover I was adopted until recently, after my parents died. They'd never told me."

Lia leaned forward. "Then you *do* understand. It
was such a shock to realize that all along my grandparents were aware of Great-aunt Marie-Louise and
also other de la Roche relatives in New Orleans." She
bit her lip. "Why did they keep it a secret from me?"

Guy, trying to regain his poise after his unintended
confession, could only mark time. "And so this letter
led to their revelation."

Lia nodded. "The de la Roches are on Gram's—my
grandmother's—side of the family, and I'm convinced she never would have admitted they existed if I
hadn't shown her the letter. For some reason she dis-
likes them. She advised me to tear up the letter and

forget about any de la Roche inheritance. 'No good ever came from that family,' she warned me."

"Did she explain her reasons?"

"Not really. Oh, she muttered something about there not being anything for me to inherit in New Orleans except darkness and trouble, but she refused to be specific."

Guy glanced at the letter again. "I assume you noticed that the bequest is contingent on you going to New Orleans and living in the mansion for a minimum of three months. How do you feel about that?"

"I wondered if I really had to do it, though I'm fairly sure I could get a three-month leave of absence from my job. I've recently trained an assistant and she could take over as the medical librarian while I'm gone. Still, I'm not certain I want to actually live there. Is there anything you can do to have that requirement thrown out?"

"First let me ask you if you really want to accept this inheritance?"

Lia stared at him across the desk, her dark eyes wide and appealing. Guy found himself thinking he'd never have enough of looking into those beautiful brown eyes, eyes familiar to him in some strange way, a way he couldn't fathom. The conviction came to him that he'd not only seen her before but somewhere, sometime he'd held her in his arms....

"I've seesawed back and forth," Lia admitted, her words jolting him back to reality. "First yes, then no, then maybe. I've finally come to the conclusion that I want to go to New Orleans and see exactly what I've inherited before I decide what to do.''

He nodded approvingly. "A wise move. Louisiana law differs from other states because its roots are French, not English, so I'd have to consult with this law firm—'' he tapped the letter with his forefinger "—DuBois, LaBranche and Charters, but I believe there's a good chance of voiding that odd contingency clause.''

"Would you do that, please?'' She smiled hesitantly. "I'm really excited about all this, even though Gram's bombshell upset me. I've never been to New Orleans and inheriting a mansion seems like some kind of wonderful dream.''

"As it happens, I'm leaving for New Orleans this evening,'' he said, "and I'll be in the city for several weeks, maybe longer. If you like, I'll be glad to meet you there. The two of us could then go together to meet with the attorney, DuBois, apparently, who's handling the estate. When do you plan to arrive?''

Lia blinked, obviously taken aback. He wondered why. Was she concerned about there being an additional charge for his services in New Orleans?

"I have a plane reservation for tomorrow morning,'' she said hesitantly, "but I wouldn't want you to go out of your way. I don't wish to interfere with your plans.''

"I assure you it won't be any trouble,'' he said, "nor will there be any extra fee. My plans are flexible and I really am interested in the outcome of your unexpected legacy. Tell me when your plane gets in and I'll meet you at the airport."

Again she hesitated before saying, "At noon. Thank you, I'd appreciate having you with me when I go to visit Mr. DuBois." She rose and all but bolted for the door.

Guy hurried after her but was barely in time to catch a glimpse of her as she closed the reception room door behind her. Almost as if she were afraid of me, he thought bemusedly.

"Do I seem threatening to you?" he asked Sadie when he was ready to leave. Sadie, some ten years his senior, had also been his father's secretary.

Sadie shook her head. "You? Never. Dentists are the only ones who scare me. Have a good trip, Guy, and a successful one."

Success would mean finding out who his birth parents were, he told himself as he got into the elevator. He could hardly wait to reach New Orleans. But instead of reviewing the steps he would take to begin his search, he found himself thinking it was also true that he could hardly wait to see Lia Courtois again.

Lia's grandparents arrived at her apartment just after eight that evening. Gramps turned on the TV to watch the news, but Gram followed her into the bedroom and hovered disapprovingly as Lia packed.

"No good will come of it," Gram said with a sigh. "My folks left New Orleans years ago for reasons they never told me and they warned me never to go back."

She put a fist over her heart. "I've got a bad feeling here that Marie-Louise meant you ill when she left you that legacy. Ask yourself why she's reaching from beyond the grave to force you to live in that old de la Roche mansion."

"Perhaps she hopes I'll come to cherish the place and not sell it," Lia said as she rolled two nightgowns together and stuffed them into the bag. "Anyway, I may not have to live there to inherit. Guy—I mean Mr. Russell, the lawyer—is looking into it."

Guy. Why did she get that unwanted quiver of anticipation when she said his name? She feared it had been a mistake to agree to meet him in New Orleans but at the same time she looked forward to seeing him again with an eagerness that upset her.

Gram shook her head, saying urgently, "None are so blind as those who refuse to see. I've dreamed of black water and of darkness, and I tell you that you're walking into a dreadful, unknown peril. Don't go, Lia."

Lia turned around and hugged her grandmother. "I've made up my mind to at least take a look at the place. Don't worry so. Nothing will happen to me. And certainly not just because you had a bad dream."

In his hotel room on the tenth floor of the New Orleans Hilton, Guy flicked off the TV and the lights. He slid down in the bed, fell asleep almost immediately and dreamed.

A woman in white glided past him, pale, lovely and ethereal, her long dark hair flowing over her shoulders and down her back. Though he couldn't see her face, he knew she was Lia. He tried to call her name so she would turn and come to him, but he couldn't speak. He tried to go after her, but he couldn't move.

Where was she going? Did she know how he longed to be with her? She must, for they were connected by invisible and unbreakable chains. He'd follow her anywhere.

This wasn't the first time she'd beckoned to him, nor would it be the last. He was aware it had happened before. With Lia? Yes, it must have been with Lia. Who else would he follow?

She turned at last, saw him, and held out her arms. He stared, not certain for a moment that she *was* Lia. But of course she must be, hadn't she always been?

She drifted toward him, hardly seeming to touch the ground. *"Zha ray ve en,"* she whispered, then repeated what she'd said. *"Zha ray ve en."*

He'd heard those nonsense words many times before and they hung between him and Lia, strange awesome words whose meaning only she understood.

He struggled to ask her what she meant and what she wanted but speech was beyond his power. He gazed longingly at her, wanting her with all his heart and soul. She had an unearthly beauty no other woman could ever match, a beauty that would lure any man to her, lure him to destruction. But destruction couldn't be what she meant for him.

As though his intense regard was too much for her to bear, she began to grow more wraithlike, dissolving. If he could, he would beg her to stay with him but he had no words, just as he had no will.

Now a woman of mist, she beckoned to him, and he knew he must go to her whether willing or not, go wherever she led. Isn't that what he wished for, didn't he yearn to follow Lia?

If she *was* Lia. He could no longer be completely sure the misty woman in white was she. What was happening was all too familiar. He'd gone through this many, many times before—watched the white wraith appear, listened to her strange words, felt the overwhelming compulsion to follow her even though she was drawing him into a darkness he mistrusted.

As always, he was torn between his desire and his fear, both wanting to be with her and wanting to flee. He was aware he had no real choice, that he'd never had any choice.

She reached a pale ghostlike hand to him and he understood all over again that once she touched him he was lost. Doomed for all time. He couldn't move, all he could do was watch her misty fingers come closer and closer....

CHAPTER TWO

Guy awoke abruptly from the nightmare, his heart racing. He sat up and, though he knew he was in a hotel room, the woman in white still haunted him. He flicked on the light, leaned back against the pillows, took a deep breath and then let it out slowly.

He hadn't had what he'd always thought of as *the Dream* for a long time. Years. But he remembered every detail very well. The only difference was that this time the dark-haired woman seemed to have Lia Courtois's face. Had she always looked like Lia? He wasn't sure.

He couldn't recall how old he'd been when the dream first plagued him, though he did remember that he'd believed the woman of mist was always waiting in the night for him. As a child, when he woke in fright his mother would be there to comfort him but he'd never been able to explain to her why his recurrent dream was so terrifying.

There'd been nights when his father would join her at his bedside, trying not to show his concern. Once, if Guy could trust his early memory, his father had said something to his mother about babies not having any befores. He hadn't understood his father's meaning at the time, he hadn't even been sure it applied to him because he'd been aware he wasn't a baby.

In the light of what he knew now—that he'd been adopted—his father's words were clear enough. Evidently his mother had been worried that his nightmares might have come from something that had happened during the time before he'd come to live with them.

Guy shook his head. According to his uncles he'd been less than a month old when he was adopted, essentially a newborn with no past. No befores. Where had *the Dream* come from, then? And, why, after years of absence, had the pale woman returned to haunt him?

Perhaps meeting Lia had triggered the dream. But had she always been in it or had he merely added her face to the woman in white? Nothing about the dream made sense. His questions had no answers.

Go back to sleep, Russell, he advised himself. Then it occurred to him that he was only a Russell by adoption. Would he keep the name if he ever discovered who his birth parents were? He couldn't answer that question, either. But he damn well meant to do everything possible to find out who he was. Starting bright and early tomorrow.

He wasn't able to fall asleep again until near dawn and, because he'd failed to set the alarm or ask for a wake-up call, he didn't rouse until close to eleven. So much for bright and early—he barely made it to the airport by noon. Luckily he'd already checked the incoming flights from San Francisco and so knew what airline she'd be on. He reached the gate just as she came out of the Arrivals tunnel, dressed, as he'd been the day before, a little too warmly for a New Orleans July but even more beautiful than he remembered. In her pale pink silk suit she stood out from the other passengers like an orchid in a bouquet of daisies.

She saw him immediately and he relaxed when she smiled at him in greeting, apparently glad he was there. In the office she'd been so hesitant to agree to their meeting that he hadn't been sure of his welcome.

While she waited for her luggage, he called DuBois, LaBranche and Charters and set up an appointment with Henry DuBois for two o'clock.

"I'm able to accommodate you only because of a last minute cancellation," the receptionist told him sternly. "Ordinarily you should call at least a week in advance, preferably two weeks."

When they reached his rental car, Guy told Lia he was staying at the Hilton and asked if she'd chosen a hotel.

"I think I'll wait until after I've seen Mr. DuBois," she said, taking off her jacket. "It may be possible for me to stay at the mansion."

Since he'd looked forward to taking her to dinner in the city and had hoped to spend the evening with her, his nod lacked enthusiasm.

The law firm's offices were at the edge of the French Quarter in a charming old Spanish-style building. As they entered, Guy caught a glimpse of a courtyard hidden from the street that ran along the side of the building. Almost immediately they were shown into Mr. DuBois's office.

The attorney, an older man with white hair and a white mustache, was talking on the phone as they entered. Without glancing at them, he waved toward the chairs near his desk. Guy seated Lia but remained standing. Moments later, DuBois replaced the phone and turned toward them. Though he'd started to smile, the smile faded as he stared at the two of them, obviously taken aback. "Mr. Revenir?" he asked, his tone incredulous.

"No," Guy said, thinking the receptionist must have forgotten to tell DuBois about the cancellation and he'd been expecting someone else. "This is Lia Courtois from Oakland. We've come to discuss the de la Roche estate she's recently inherited. I'm her attorney, Guy Russell." He held out his hand.

"Yes, yes, of course," DuBois said, shaking his hand. "Sorry for the confusion." He smiled at Lia. "Delighted to meet you, my dear. When they told me you were coming in to see me I was so pleased to hear you were in the city." He nodded at Guy. "Do be seated, Mr. Russell. It's always a pleasure to greet a fellow attorney."

Realizing that DuBois had been aware they were coming, after all, Guy wondered why the man had seemed so surprised. Perhaps he'd momentarily forgotten.

After the initial pleasantries were over, Guy immediately got down to business. "Ms. Courtois has asked me to question the three-month residence clause you mentioned to her in your letter. What are the chances of having it voided?"

DuBois steepled his hands and paused a moment or two before replying. "I tried to dissuade Miss de la Roche from making such a requirement but, although not at all senile, she *was* somewhat eccentric. She insisted it be put in. Your chances of having the requirement voided are quite good, I believe. Unfortunately, as I'm sure you realize, Mr. Russell, our court agendas are extremely crowded. By the time the issue could be raised in court, the three months would be well past. Unless Ms. Courtois feels very strongly about complying, it would save everyone's time if she simply meets the requirement. Although I'm not advising this. No, not at all."

He glanced at Lia. "You do understand what I'm saying, don't you, my dear?"

She nodded, then said, "I'd rather not make any decisions until I see the estate. When may I?"

"As soon as you wish," DuBois said. "Today, if you like, although, unfortunately, I shan't be able to come along."

"I'll take Ms. Courtois to the estate," Guy put in.

"Very good. The place is some miles upriver from the city. I'll see that you're given directions. There's a housekeeper in residence at the mansion so you'll have no difficulty entering."

"Do you think the housekeeper is prepared to have me spend the night?" Lia asked.

"If that's what you'd like to do, I shouldn't think that would pose a problem. But, before we go any further, I will require your signature on a few papers, Ms. Courtois, as well as the copy of your birth certificate and the other papers that I asked you to supply."

"I have them with me," Lia said.

The legalities were quickly completed. As she got to her feet, Lia asked, "What was my Great-aunt Marie-Louise like, Mr. DuBois? I never met her."

DuBois rose and glanced away from her toward the courtyard visible from his office windows. For a long moment he seemed to study a large bush with bright red blooms next to the window, then he turned back to her. "I fear that's a difficult question to answer. Marie-Louise de la Roche was not an easy woman to know. Sulie Mason, her old housekeeper, will be able to tell you far more than I can, I'm sure. If it's of any interest to you, I believe I can see a rather marked resemblance between you and Marie-Louise as a young woman."

Lia smiled uncertainly. "Thank you for your time," she said, holding out her hand.

"I'm at your disposal." He took her hand and bowed slightly over it rather than shaking it. He glanced at Guy and murmured something that sounded like, "Most remarkable."

Before Guy could ask him what he meant, a voice on the intercom said, "I'm sorry to interrupt but Mr. Beasley is on line one, Mr. DuBois."

"It's been my pleasure to meet you both," DuBois said, ushering them to the door. "I wish I had more time but I'm sure you understand, counselor. My secretary, Ms. Kittridge, will supply you with directions to the estate and will also call to let the housekeeper know you'll be arriving."

When they were in the car on their way to the estate, Lia at first kept her comments to what she saw as they drove along—the height of the levees, the above-ground tombs in the cemeteries, the white egrets at an ornamental pool in a small park. Guy began to wonder if she intended to discuss the estate at all.

As they crossed the Mississippi on the Huey P. Long Bridge, she leaned back in her seat and, looking straight ahead rather than at him, asked, "Why do you think Mr. DuBois wouldn't tell me anything about my great-aunt? I'm sure he knew more than he said."

Guy had no doubt she was right but he wasn't certain DuBois's reticence was all that remarkable. "Lawyers tend to be cautious, you know," he said.

"I suppose. But I had a feeling that he made a decision to hold something back that I should know."

Glancing at her, he met her troubled gaze and saw she was really disturbed. "What's upsetting you?" he asked.

"Sometimes I get these flashes of what Gram calls 'reading the atmosphere.' Her words pretty well describe what happened in Mr. DuBois's office. The atmosphere, if you want to call it that, was skewed from the moment we walked in. First he stared at you as though he'd seen a ghost and then he called you by the wrong name. What do you think that was all about?"

About to mention they'd taken the place of someone who'd canceled an appointment, Guy blinked as it struck him that there might have been another reason entirely. DuBois might have called him Mr. Revenir because he actually looked like whoever Revenir might be. If he did have a resemblance to this Revenir, that could explain why DuBois muttered, "Most remarkable."

Excitement thrummed through Guy. Could this be a clue to his origins? He would contact DuBois as soon as he had the chance and question him. But he was reluctant to share his thoughts about this intriguing possibility with Lia in case he was way off base.

"What else bothered you about the meeting with DuBois?" he asked her.

"He must have known *why* my great-aunt insisted on me living in the mansion for three months, even though he advised against putting it into the will. But he very carefully avoided telling me what her reason was."

"Did you feel he was pushing you to go ahead and do as she asked?"

"I felt he was warning me off. Didn't you get the impression he doesn't want me to stay in the mansion?"

Guy shook his head. "You must be more sensitive to nuances than I am."

"He not only didn't want me in the mansion, he didn't want me in his office. He got rid of us as quickly as he could."

"Attorneys usually have fairly tight schedules," Guy pointed out. "I know I do."

Lia shook her head. "That wasn't the reason. I'm not sure what his reason could be but I suspect seeing me in person made him feel guilty in some way or other." She shot him a speculative glance. "Convinced you have a nut case on your hands?"

Guy grinned at her. "Not yet. Keep talking and I'll let you know when you cross the line."

She smiled. "It's really very good of you to go to all this trouble. The mansion is miles out of your way, I'm sure."

"After hearing everything in DuBois's office, I'm almost as eager to see the old place as you are. Pre-Civil War, didn't Ms. Kittridge say? If the mansion hasn't been kept up, maybe DuBois is worried that the roof might fall in on you."

So far he'd been successful in keeping more or less to his client-attorney mode with Lia, concentrating on her inheritance rather than on her, shutting out the powerful flow of chemistry between them. How long he could keep it up was another matter. Despite the car's air-conditioning he kept catching faint whiffs of the floral scent she wore, one he couldn't identify but one he certainly did appreciate.

Her silk skirt didn't quite reach her knees and he had difficulty keeping his gaze from what was revealed. He'd been very careful not to touch her. If he touched her, he'd be lost. Which reminded him of his dream.

"I may have dreamed about you last night," he found himself saying, realizing too late that he'd spoken out loud.

Okay, so he'd just proven he was an idiot, after all. "Into the head and out through the mouth is a fool's way," his mother used to warn. "Intelligent people think it over before they speak."

Lia turned in her seat, giving him her full attention. "May have? How odd. Don't you know?"

"Not really," he admitted, feeling more foolish by the minute.

"You're going to have to explain that."

This time he did think, editing the dream before speaking. "It's an old dream, a recurrent one that goes back to when I was a little kid. There's always been a beautiful, if somewhat misty, woman in my dream, a dark-haired woman who wants me to follow her somewhere. Last night that woman had your face. At least, I think she did."

"What you're telling me is that I may or may not be the woman of your dreams. Are lawyers always so indecisive?" Amusement threaded through her words.

"Cautious, maybe, but I deny indecisive."

"No, counselor, I've got the corner on caution, look before you leap and all that."

"There's enough left over for me. So, what do you suggest we two cautious people do?"

"Remain that way."

He shook his head. "Not forever. I've thought of a solution. Look before you leap? No need to look. What we'll do is hold hands, close our eyes and jump over the brink together."

"Landing where?" she asked dryly.

He shrugged and slanted a sly look her way. "Who cares?"

Guy's glance was so expressive that he didn't need to add they wouldn't care because, wherever it was, they'd be there together. For a moment Lia let herself imagine the two of them hand in hand, eyes shut, taking that most dangerous leap of all....

But of course she'd learned better, learned the hard way. She shouldn't have let down her guard with Guy, not even partway. Unfortunately she found it all too easy. What woman could sit next to him and not be aware of his attractiveness? Or his incredibly potent masculinity? How could she be expected to keep ignoring the current sparking between them, there whether she willed it or not? And, damn it, she was actually beginning to like him for reasons that had nothing to do with chemistry.

"Do you mind if I turn on the radio?" she asked, hoping to distract herself. She didn't want to think about Guy nor did she wish to ask herself unanswerable questions about the estate. Not until she'd seen it.

"Why not?" Guy said. "Maybe we can sing along. Cautiously, of course."

She gave him a mock glare and flicked on the radio. Searching for a station, she came to one that played country western, and he immediately began singing the words to the song, something about false women and true but bleeding hearts. Grimacing, she listened a moment or two and then, refusing to be outdone, joined in.

Eventually she switched to another station that featured sentimental ballads and they sang those, too, using the commercial breaks to chide one another for having terrible musical taste.

When at last they came to the pillars Ms. Kittridge had told them to look for—griffins, one with its left wing broken off, set on massive blocks of stone—Lia switched off the radio and they drove between the pillars onto a gravel drive in fair condition. Lia's hopes rose. Perhaps she would find everything else in decent enough shape, too.

For a time the drive wound between tall trees that formed a canopy overhead—live oaks? She wasn't sure. Then suddenly the mansion itself came into view and she drew in her breath, both impressed and dismayed. Though the stately, columned house still retained elegance, its once white paint had chipped and faded, revealing bare wood in places. Some of the black shutters hung askew and others were missing entirely. A large section of the roof obviously needed repair.

"How sad," Guy said. "Like a beautiful woman gone to ruin."

Lia took offense. "Determination and money can fix up both women and houses," she said sharply.

Instead of responding directly, he merely commented, "The shrubbery's been allowed to run so wild the grounds are a jungle."

She ignored his words, true though they were, feeling subtly drawn to the place and not wanting to listen to criticism. If she decided to stay here, all that she'd noticed so far could be changed, could be brought back to how it was meant to be. She yearned to get started but knew she would have to wait until the house was really hers.

"I wonder if it has a name," she mused, as Guy pulled the car around the looped drive and stopped in front of the house. "We should have asked Mr. DuBois."

"The housekeeper is sure to know," Guy said, getting out and stretching.

Not waiting for him to come around to her side, she opened her door, slid from the car and walked hesitantly up wobbly steps to the porch. Lifting the iron knocker, she let it fall once, twice, three times against the striker plate. For what seemed like a very long time, nothing happened.

Guy, who'd joined her on the porch, said, "We might have better luck at the back."

She knew his suggestion was logical yet she didn't want to follow it. For some reason it was important to her to enter this house—her house—for the first time through the front door. She was reaching for the knocker again when the door creaked open a crack and a white-haired woman peered at her.

"I'm Lia Courtois," she announced.

The old woman glanced from her to Guy and back, saying nothing.

"You must be Sulie Mason," Lia said. "Didn't Mr. DuBois tell you I was coming?"

Muttering something unintelligible about the phone, the old woman opened the door all the way. "Come in, come in, do, Miss Lia," she said in a musical voice that belied her age. In contrast to her white hair, her wrinkled skin was a deep, warm brown. "Reason it took me so long is we don't be using the front door. Everybody pretty much comes in the back way. 'Sides, you took me by surprise, you did." She glanced at Guy, then quickly away. "Him, more than you. Didn't be expecting him, and that's the truth."

"My name's Guy Russell. I'm Ms. Courtois's attorney," Guy told the housekeeper.

"Must be you couldn't help coming here," she said to him, shaking her head. "Too bad, too bad." She turned again to Lia. "I got a room all fixed for you, just waiting for you. Where's your bags?"

Lia, who hadn't been entirely sure she intended to stay, realized she'd made up her mind as soon as she saw the house. "My things are in the car. But, before you show me to my room, I'd like to take a quick look through the house."

"You take your time looking," Sulie said. "I got some gumbo simmering in the kitchen. That's where I'll be do you want me." She walked away with a youthful spring to her step that amazed Lia.

"She must be at least in her eighties," she said to Guy in a low tone, "but she moves like a teenager."

"She certainly didn't take to me," he said ruefully.

Lia frowned. "That *was* odd, what she said to you. But it probably doesn't mean anything." Her face cleared, and, without thinking, she reached for his hand. "Come on, let's explore!"

When his fingers closed over hers, Lia felt the shock of the contact tingle along every nerve in her body. He stood as still as she, staring into her eyes, making her aware that he felt the same disturbing, inexplicable thrill. His golden eyes, she saw, had tiny brown flecks in them. He tugged at her hand, pulling her to him, and she went willingly, unable to resist.

His lips brushed hers, tentatively at first, almost as though he feared to kiss her. Then he gathered her into his arms, his mouth covering hers hungrily. She matched his hunger with her own. It had been so long since he'd held her, so very, very long....

How can that be? Lia thought in confusion, bemused by the power of his kiss. Why do I think about how long it's been when Guy has never kissed me before?

Suddenly he thrust her away from him. "Not me," he rasped, as though in answer.

Her hand flew to her mouth where she could still feel the imprint of his kiss. She stared at him in stupefaction.

He leaned against the wall as though needing its support. "How did it happen?" He seemed to be asking himself as much as her.

"What did you mean when you said it wasn't you?" she demanded, her confusion diminishing.

"I'm not sure. I felt—driven." He straightened, took a deep breath and eased it out. "You must know how attractive you are and God knows I've wanted to kiss you, but just now—" He shook his head. "Crazy as it sounds, it didn't seem as though *I* was kissing you."

Lia nodded uncertainly. She wasn't altogether sure she understood what he meant, but, though she could still feel the effect of that kiss throughout her entire body, she too had been aware something was wrong.

Guy looked around as if expecting to find an answer written on the paneled walls of the entry. "You can't stay here," he said harshly. "Not after that."

Lia bridled. "Why not? What happened between us has nothing to do with the house. I felt it before, back in Oakland in your—" She broke off abruptly, wishing she could swallow what she'd already admitted. But it was too late.

He nodded slowly. "I felt something there, too. You have a point."

Instead of his words reassuring Lia, it frightened her to realize he'd experienced the same unsettling sensations that she'd had in his Oakland office. Whatever it was, they were in it together.

"I still don't like the idea of you staying alone out here," he said. "It's more isolated than I thought it would be."

"I'm not alone. Sulie's with me. And I'm not afraid." She stretched out her arms. "I'm welcome in this house. I can feel I am, and I intend to stay here."

"Overnight? Or longer?"

"Maybe for the three months, if I can arrange it. Mr. DuBois said I might as well because it would take longer than that to void the requirement."

"You told me earlier he tried to discourage you."

Lia shrugged. "Don't worry, I'll be perfectly safe overnight. We can discuss my plans at another time. Right now I'm going to get my bags out of your car so you can return to the city." She walked to the front door and opened it.

As Guy started to follow her, he realized nothing he could say was going to change her mind, at least about tonight. He also realized his reluctance to leave her here was unreasonable. Sulie had stayed on alone without any problems after Marie-Louise de la Roche died, why should anything happen to Lia with the two of them here?

Yet Guy couldn't shake the feeling that he shouldn't go, that he ought to stay and make sure she was safe.

He was startled by Sulie's voice coming from behind him. "Best go while you still can," she advised him. "The longer you be staying, the harder it be to go, till you find you can't leave this place. Best go now."

He turned to her. "I don't understand what you mean. Are you telling me that you don't want me here?"

"Don't make no never mind what I be wanting. Ain't got nothing to do with what I say to you. She got you here, I can see that plain, and she means to keep you here."

CHAPTER THREE

As Guy drove back into the city, he tried to make sense of Sulie's rambling. When he'd attempted to question her about what she meant, all he got from the housekeeper was that "Ole Miss" had made her promise not to tell. Ole Miss was evidently Marie-Louise de la Roche.

"She swear she come back from beyond and haunt me, do I tell," Sulie had insisted. "So me, I don't be telling, not to no one."

Guy had disliked leaving Lia behind but she'd proved as stubborn about what she meant to do as Sulie had been about providing information, so he'd finally torn himself away. That's exactly what it had felt like, a ripping away. Part of him still wanted to turn the car around and hurry back to Lia.

With an effort, he banished Lia and the estate from his thoughts, reminding himself of the reason he'd come to New Orleans. Glancing at his watch, he decided he ought to be able to catch the senior partner, DuBois, before he left his office and question him about that Mr. Revenir mistake.

* * *

Ms. Kittridge was rising from her desk, her shoulder bag in hand when he entered the office. "Why, Mr. Russell," she said. "I do hope my directions didn't get you lost."

"They were very good," he said. "We had no problem finding the estate. I came back here in the hope I might have a word with Mr. DuBois before he left for the day. It will only take a minute or two."

"Oh, I'm so sorry—you've missed him. And I'm afraid he hasn't just left for the day, but for three weeks in Europe." She glanced at her watch. "His flight was scheduled to depart a half hour ago. Is this anything Mr. LaBranche or Mr. Charters might help you with?"

Guy hesitated. Could they? He doubted it. What had happened was between DuBois and himself. Besides, he might be completely wrong in his interpretation of what DuBois had meant. "I don't think so, thanks."

He left the office feeling let down. This is New Orleans, he chided himself as he drove toward the Hilton. The Big Easy, one of the most colorful cities in America. Give the place a chance. You haven't even visited the French Quarter yet and there's the entire evening and the night ahead of you. Enjoy yourself.

Later, wandering on foot through the Quarter, he was distracted for a while by marching jazz bands, jugglers performing on street corners and the artists congregated around Jackson Square. He dropped in to Miss Ruby's for jambalaya and found himself sharing a table, family-style. Since the man across from him proved to be a compulsive talker, by the time Guy finished eating, he was as full of New Orleans trivia as he was New Orleans food.

"It's a fact," the man called after him as he started to leave. "Not only is Canal Street the widest in the country but New Orleans is the only major city without a street named Main."

New Orleans *was* different, Guy reflected as he walked along St. Louis Street. Not due to the width of Canal Street nor the lack of a Main Street but because he could almost believe he was in another country. It was a fascinating city. What made my birth mother leave here? he asked himself. He wondered if she'd once walked where he was walking now. Had she crossed Jackson Square? Stood on the levee and watched the brown waters of the Mississippi flow toward the Gulf?

Father unknown. Was that true or had she, for some reason, refused to name the man responsible? Would he ever know anything about either of them?

"Let sleeping dogs lie," Uncle Tim had advised. "Should you chance to discover your origins, you may not like what you find."

He turned a corner without noticing what street he was on. After two more turns, his attention was caught by a display in a store window, a large twisted root. As he gazed at it, he saw the figures of a man and a woman, the two so intricately entwined that it was impossible to know where one left off and the other began. The longer he stared, the more certain he became that he was the man and the woman was Lia. He blinked and looked again—at a twisted root.

"You interested in a love potion, sir?" a voice asked.

Shrugging off his uneasiness at what he'd imagined he'd seen, Guy glanced at the dark-skinned man lounging in the open doorway to the shop.

After an assessing look at Guy the man smiled and shook his head. "You don't need no love potion, for sure. But we got whatever you do need—amulets, St. John's root, ask and ye shall be supplied."

Guy pointed at the window display. "Is that St. John's root?"

"That's mandrake, biggest I ever seen. Mandrake's magic, you know. Folks tell me they see all different things in that root. Me, I see Damballah coiling, storing up power for the time he gets loose. Man, what a time that's gonna be."

Guy hadn't the least idea what he was talking about. Voodoo, maybe—after all this *was* New Orleans. "Thanks," he said, "but I don't need anything."

He continued on, but, while he could shrug off the root, he couldn't easily dismiss Lia from his mind, nor what had happened between them before he left the mansion. He'd been deeply aroused by their brief embrace and at the same time he'd sensed a wrongness, a feeling he'd been manipulated into kissing her. Not by Lia, but by—what? It didn't make any sense.

Just the same, he'd sure as hell enjoyed the kiss while it lasted.

At the mansion, despite Sulie's objections, Lia helped clean up after the evening meal. "I couldn't possibly cook gumbo as delicious as yours but I can certainly wipe dishes," she told the housekeeper as she lifted a towel from a rack attached to the end of a cupboard.

"I'm not used to being waited on, you know," Lia continued. "My parents were killed in an accident when I was a baby and my grandparents raised me. From the time I was quite small I was expected to pitch in and help."

Sulie nodded. "Your grandmama's daddy was a de la Roche, Ole Miss say."

Lia sighed. "Gram never spoke of her relatives. In fact, I didn't even know I had any besides my grandparents until the letter came from Mr. DuBois. I'm sorry I wasn't able to meet my great-aunt before she died."

"Just as well," Sulie said. "Ole Miss wasn't what you call easy."

"It was wonderful of her to leave me her estate."

"Maybe. Maybe not."

Lia glanced at her curiously. "How could it not be good?"

"Ole Miss be dead and gone now. Gonna be trouble soon as he comes back."

"I don't understand what you mean. As soon as who comes back?"

"That man you be bringing here with you."

"Guy Russell? I don't know that he *is* coming back. Even if he does happen to visit me before he returns to Oakland, Guy has nothing to do with the de la Roches."

Sulie squeezed the dish mop dry and hung it on a hook above the old white porcelain sink, then poured the dishpan water down the drain. The kitchen, though functional, was anything but modern.

Fixing her gaze on Lia, she said, "Mr. Guy, he can't help but come back here. You wait and see."

Believing Sulie must have seen them kiss, Lia shook her head, flushing a little. "If you think he's interested in me, the truth is we hardly know each other. Actually, Guy came to New Orleans on business that has nothing to do with me or this estate."

Sulie turned away and began placing the clean dishes in the cupboard. Lia had already discovered that the old housekeeper, while friendly, wouldn't answer every question asked of her. Apparently Sulie had said all she was going to about Guy.

Lia was surprised at how strong her hope was that he would return soon. Because she was eager to show him through the mansion, she told herself. She'd explored the first and second floors, amazed at the antique treasures in the rooms, feeling as though she were in a museum. Overwhelmed, she hadn't gone on to look in the attic or ask about any outbuildings. She already knew there was no cellar.

"Dig down and you quick come to water," Sulie had explained. "Can't be burying people in the ground hereabouts, on account of that water they rise up. We got to shut the dead up in tombs."

Which explained the aboveground crypts she'd already noticed in the New Orleans cemeteries. No doubt her great-aunt had been buried in one of them. She must ask Sulie where and visit Marie-Louise's grave.

"Does your room suit you?" Sulie asked. "We can change you to another real easy."

"I love my room," Lia assured her. It was the truth. She was no furniture expert but she did recognize Louis Quatorze style when she saw it and she had a hunch the delicate white-and-gold bedroom suite in her room might be genuine. "Everything is exquisite." She frowned as she remembered what was pinned to the wall above her bed. "Except for that odd bunch of feathers attached to a bone by my bed. Why is it there?"

"That be gris-gris to protect you while you sleep."

"Gris-gris? What on earth is that?"

"Amulet, some say."

"Did you put it there?"

Sulie nodded.

Since Sulie obviously meant it for the best, Lia didn't pursue the subject. She wasn't superstitious enough to believe in the power of amulets but she realized she'd have to leave the unlovely object where it was or hurt Sulie's feelings.

Later, as she undressed for bed, she ignored the gris-gris, wondering if she was going to be able to sleep in this heat. White curtains shimmied in the slight breeze from the open windows, a breeze that did nothing to cool the room. The fan on the dressing table whirred back and forth, stirring the warm air but giving only the illusion of coolness. She thought of Guy in his air-conditioned room at the Hilton and sighed, momentarily envious.

Still, even with the heat, she was glad she'd decided to stay in the mansion. Her mansion, though she hadn't yet gotten used to the idea. Would she ever be able to persuade her grandparents to come here? How she would love to show them what she'd inherited.

She pulled the covers back, climbed into the bed, then clicked off the bedside lamp. The silver gleam of a waxing moon peeked through a gap in the curtains, dimly illuminating the room. She closed her eyes, intending to plan what she'd do tomorrow but thoughts of Guy pushed everything else from her mind.

Though she didn't want to remember that strange, haunting kiss in the foyer, she couldn't stop herself from reliving every exciting moment. No man had ever kissed her quite so passionately, nor had she ever reacted quite so intensely. When she found that just thinking about the kiss aroused her and that she'd begun to wish Guy was here with her now, Lia rose from the bed and padded to the window. Pushing the curtains aside, she gazed into the night, darker as well as far warmer than in Oakland.

Something white fluttered toward her window. Not a bird—what was it? A moment later she drew back as a large white moth flattened itself against the screen and clung there as though staring in to spy on her. Though she chided herself for an overactive imagination, Lia let the curtains fall into place and left the window. She climbed back into bed, flicked on the light and picked up one of the paperbacks she'd brought along, intending to read herself to sleep.

In his hotel room Guy fell asleep quickly, only to rouse again and again, certain someone had called his name. A woman. Lia? Each time he woke it took him a moment or two to realize he was alone. His sleep was restless and he awoke in the morning feeling apprehensive. Was Lia all right? Unable to wait to find out, he picked up the phone and punched in her number. Nothing happened, no ring, no busy signal.

After repeated tries he called the operator and when she couldn't get any response she advised him to notify the phone company's service department. He did so, quelling an urgent need to fling on his clothes and rush to the mansion.

There's no reason to believe Lia's in trouble, he told himself firmly. Her phone's out of order, that's all. Come to think of it, the phone might not have been working yesterday, either, when Ms. Kittridge had tried to call Sulie. That would explain Sulie's surprise at seeing them. She *had* muttered something about the phone, something he hadn't quite caught.

He would go to the mansion, yes, but later, after he took care of his own business. Sometime during last night's walk he'd decided how to go about the search. Glancing at his watch he saw it was too early to expect to contact anyone in an office. He had plenty of time to wash, dress and have breakfast first.

Near ten, he phoned Ms. Kittridge, told her what he needed and she connected him with Mr. LaBranche. Once Guy had explained who he was and described his meeting with Mr. DuBois the previous day, Bob LaBranche proved most helpful. Guy hung up with an invitation to have lunch sometime and the names of three private investigators that DuBois, LaBranche and Charters had found reliable.

Guy chose the second name on the list, Lawrence Lafitte, for no reason other than a man with the same last name as an infamous New Orleans pirate fit his notion of a P.I. Before he left for his appointment with Lafitte, he packed his belongings and checked out of the hotel, telling himself he'd find a place closer to the de la Roche mansion.

Mr. Lafitte—"call me Larry"—turned out to be slim, of average height, and balding. He wasn't a man anyone would look at twice, which, on reflection, Guy realized was a plus for a person in his business.

After listening to Guy, Lafitte opened Jane Doe's gold locket and studied the woman's picture inside.

"Mind if I keep this for a few days?" he asked. "I'll give you a receipt."

"No problem."

Lafitte studied him for a moment. "You realize you haven't given me much to go on—this locket, your uncle having once heard that your pregnant mother, known only as Jane Doe, came from New Orleans and the fact that Henry DuBois called you Mr. Revenir. Too bad he's in Europe. We might be able to reach him there but I don't advise it because I can probably find out about the Revenir business without going to that expense. Mind if I take your picture?"

"Go ahead."

Lafitte took three shots, two frontal and a profile. "I'll do my best," he told Guy afterwards, "but don't expect miracles."

Aware that Lafitte had far more resources than he did for such a search, Guy left the office satisfied. Once back in his car, he immediately headed for the mansion. Slowed by traffic, he chafed, unable to convince himself there was no need to hurry.

When he finally did arrive, recalling how Sulie had said everyone used the back door, he drove toward the rear of the house where he found a white sports car, one of the expensive foreign makes, parked near the back entrance.

Sulie answered his knock, shaking her head when she saw him. "Too bad you come back," she muttered as she let him into the kitchen. "Miss Lia's in the morning room, she be talking to Miss Rebecca."

"Who's Miss Rebecca?"

"Rebecca de la Roche, she be a cousin to Miss Lia. She come just ahead of you. Best you go in and hear why she come, you being Miss Lia's lawyer."

Following Sulie's pointing finger, Guy made his way along a short hall to a closed door on his right. He tapped on it. Lia opened the door, gave him a smile that made his heart leap, and invited him in.

As Lia made the introductions, he noticed that Rebecca was a darkly attractive, fortyish woman. She was obviously jittery and he wondered why. After nodding to her, he took the seat Lia waved him to and turned down her offer of ice tea.

"Since you're Lia's attorney," Rebecca said, "I imagine she doesn't mind if I speak freely in front of you."

"Go right ahead," Lia put in.

"Well, of course, some of my reason for coming here today was pure curiosity," Rebecca said. "I was interested in meeting my California cousin face-to-face." She glanced at Guy. "Charming, isn't she?"

"All the de la Roche women I've met appear to be charming," he told her.

Rebecca's smile was forced. "A gallant attorney, how lovely." She picked up the woven fan resting in her lap and waved it front of her. "Cousin Lia, if you intend to remain here you really should install air-conditioning. Dear Aunt Marie-Louise was stubbornly old-fashioned but there's no reason you can't bring the old place up-to-date."

"I'm not sure of my plans at the moment," Lia said.

Rebecca leaned forward tensely. "I do hope you haven't had any problems."

"No, not really." Lia sounded as puzzled as Guy felt.

Why was Rebecca on edge? he asked himself again.

"Good!" Rebecca sounded genuinely pleased. "I sincerely hope you'll stay. After all, you're here more or less at my instigation. Marie-Louise intended me to be her heir, you know, but I persuaded her otherwise."

"You told Miss de la Roche to leave the estate to Lia?" Guy asked bluntly.

"Exactly. I didn't want a white elephant on my hands, I'm quite comfortable in my own home. I certainly wouldn't want to live here, I wouldn't have been able to find it in my heart to sell the old family place and it certainly can't be rented. So, I told Marie-Louise that perhaps it was time to forgive and forget, to right old wrongs."

"I'm afraid I don't understand," Lia said.

"Perhaps you don't know the family history. At some time in the past, men being the lustful animals they are—" she slanted a glance at Guy "—the de la Roches split into two branches. Mine, legitimate. Yours, illegitimate."

As Lia stared at her, Guy said, "You're claiming my client is not legitimately a de la Roche?"

Rebecca waved the hand not holding the fan. "It's a fact but it's also of no concern all these years later. The bastard branch never did inherit, though. I told Marie-Louise so few de la Roches were left that she ought to bring those from the wrong side of the blanket into the fold."

"How many more of us bastards are there?" Lia asked. Though her voice was calm, Guy sensed the undercurrent of hostility.

"I see I've offended you." Rebecca shrugged. "It can't be helped. You were the only one Marie-Louise chose to recognize so the estate is all yours." Looking at Guy, she added, "You can be sure I shall never contest the will, counselor. Why should I? I don't want the place and, anyway, it was my idea that Lia should inherit."

Tucking her fan into her bag, she rose. "So pleasant to meet you both but I do have to run, I'm so fearfully busy. Don't bother to see me out, Lia. Do call me sometime, if you care to." Rebecca opened the door and vanished into the hall.

Lia looked at Guy. "She didn't answer my question about other relatives."

"I'd say Cousin Rebecca raised more questions than she answered," he told her, hearing the sports car rev up and roar off as he spoke.

"How do you feel about having a client from the bastard branch?" she asked.

He grinned at her. "Don't ask me. I'm a person who never could understand how anyone could tell which side of the blanket was the wrong one."

"I suppose Rebecca was telling the truth."

"I'll check into the illegitimacy part but we may never know whether or not she really did convince Marie-Louise to make you the heir. One thing did puzzle me—why was Cousin Rebecca so nervous?"

Neither of them noticed Sulie standing in the open doorway until she spoke. "That one, she be scared to come here now that Ole Miss is dead."

"But why?" Lia asked.

Sulie shook her head. "Can't say. Ole Miss told me not to." She fixed her gaze on Guy. "You be staying?" she asked. "I fixed you a room, in case."

"Oh, yes, do, Guy!" Lia cried. A moment later she blinked, as though startled by her own enthusiastic invitation.

He equivocated, giving her a chance to change her mind. "Well, I *was* planning to find a motel closer to the estate."

"Then why not stay here?" Lia asked.

"He ain't gonna say no," Sulie assured her. "Be too late for no."

In a way, Guy thought, Sulie was right. He wanted to be with Lia; he had an almost desperate need to be with her that he didn't really understand.

When he brought his bag in from the car he found that, with eight other bedrooms to choose from, Sulie had given him the room across from Lia's.

Lia, who'd followed him up the stairs, looked in and said, "I think of this bedroom as Lafayette's." She nodded to a gold-framed painting of the French general hanging on the paneled wall opposite the windows.

Guy glanced at the substantial mahogany furniture and the red-and-gold decor. "It was meant for a man, certainly." Looking back at the painting, he asked, "Have you discovered the rogue's gallery of your ancestors yet? These old mansions usually have them."

Lia frowned. "This one doesn't. In fact, I haven't seen a single painting of a de la Roche anywhere. Of course, there could be some stored in the attic—I haven't tackled that yet."

"What about your great-aunt's room? Any pictures there?"

She shook her head. "Not even a photograph album. The room doesn't look as though anyone ever used it. Sulie said Marie-Louise had her burn a lot of papers before she died. She'd already given most of her clothes to a charity. It's almost as though she didn't want anything of hers to survive her."

"I take it she never married."

"Sulie says young Marie-Louise didn't have much use for men and the older she got, the more she despised them. According to Sulie, my great-aunt didn't much like women, either. Or children. She didn't even keep a pet."

"A real loner."

"Yes, except for Sulie. They've been together for fifty years. I would have thought she'd make a provision for Sulie in the will but she didn't, except to ask that the estate pay her salary until I took over. I'll certainly keep Sulie on as long as she wants to stay and also offer her some of the money she deserves for her long service when the estate is settled. I'll have to hire more help if I decide to stay. At the moment there's only Sulie and a cleaning firm that provides a crew once a month. The laundry is sent out weekly to a company that picks it up and returns it."

"I'll look into seeing if the estate will foot the bill for extra help," Guy said. "You certainly could use a gardener or two."

"And then some. I haven't had the chance to explore the grounds yet—maybe we can do it this evening. Right now I want you to see the rest of the house."

As they walked slowly through the rooms, Lia enthused over the furnishings and it became obvious to Guy that she'd fallen in love with the old place. "Will you return to Oakland after the three months are up?" he asked as casually as he could, hiding his anger over the possibility he might never see her again.

She bit her lip. "I suppose I'll have to. There's my grandparents, for one thing. And my job. But I'm not sure I'll want to remain in Oakland."

He didn't press her any further, aware that this wasn't the moment.

After touring the first and second floors, Lia paused before a door near the main staircase. "This room is kept locked," she said, "and Sulie insists there's no key. I confess I peeked through the keyhole and found the room is empty of furnishings—not even any curtains or carpet. Sulie claims 'Ole Miss' said the room was never to be unlocked and used."

"You don't know why?"

Lia shook her head. "Sulie tends to be close-mouthed. Let's forget the room for now—I want to view the attic. Who knows what treasures are up there." Her voice was bright with anticipation.

Even before they reached the top of the narrow stairs, the heat all but stifled them. Guy expected to see an impossible clutter of discards and memorabilia and he hoped Lia didn't intend to plow through the lot today. It was just too damned hot.

He blinked in surprise when he climbed high enough to see the attic floor. Except for two trunks and an old pine wardrobe, the attic was empty. "Your great-aunt apparently cleaned house here, too," he said.

"Maybe there's something interesting in the trunks," Lia said.

He sighed, resigning himself to a search through the trunks and the wardrobe, considering himself lucky Marie-Louise had been so thorough.

One trunk held a moth-eaten Confederate officer's uniform, his sword and an ancient, rusted pistol. The other trunk was full of wrapped *objets d'art*, probably quite valuable. Guy was glad Lia didn't seem interested in looking at more than one or two. Now there was only the wardrobe and then they could get out of this furnace-hot attic.

When Lia opened the wardrobe, he drew in his breath, forgetting the heat as he stared at the single garment inside—long and filmy and white. He knew, without knowing how he knew, that it was the gown his dream woman wore.

Lia fingered the sheer material. "How lovely," she said. "It's an old-fashioned nightgown in surprisingly good condition. I'll bet it would fit me. I'll take—"

"Leave the thing where it is!" The words burst from him, beyond his control, his voice rasping with fear for Lia. "Don't touch it. And never, ever, even think of wearing that gown."

CHAPTER FOUR

"You don't go near the bayou out back," Sulie called from the rear door as Lia and Guy strolled away from the house that evening. "There be swamp by that bayou, maybe snakes."

"We're only going into the side garden and we'll stay on the paths," Lia assured her.

"If the idea of snakes bothers you, we can wait until morning to explore the grounds," Guy said.

She shook her head. "Sulie didn't say there'd be any danger except near the bayou and, anyway, it's still light enough to see what's in front of us. Besides, don't the experts say that snakes try to avoid humans?"

"I'm no expert but it sounds reasonable. We're a dangerous species. Killers, one and all."

She slanted him a look. "Speak for yourself."

"It's true. All human beings are capable of killing if the right occasion arises. Fortunately for the survival of the species, most of us would only kill to save ourselves or someone we love but the potential's there, all the same."

Lia thought over his words, decided he might have a point, and sighed. "How depressing."

"I'll admit it's not the best kind of conversation for a warm Louisiana night while strolling with a beautiful heiress through her scented gardens."

Did he really think she was beautiful? Like many men, he probably said it by reflex to any woman who interested him. Lia pushed aside the branch of an overgrown shrub, detaching one of its red blooms. Guy scooped the flower off the weedy path and offered it to her. She cupped the flower in her hand and sniffed it.

"The perfume we smell isn't from this flower," she said. "More likely jasmine—nothing smells quite so sweet as jasmine. I wonder where it is? Everything's gone so wild that we can't see the garden for the trees. And the shrubs. They're in dire need of pruning."

Guy nodded. "I'll try to get you an okay from someone at the law firm to hire at least one gardener at the estate's expense but I'm afraid it'll take time."

They walked in silence for a few moments before she said, "You still haven't really explained why you didn't want me to touch that nightgown in the attic. I don't understand what your dreams have to do with it."

"I've already told you all I could." He peered into the dusk. "What's that building up ahead?"

Though she knew he was deliberately changing the subject, Lia shrugged and followed his gaze. "Can it be a gazebo? Yes, it is!" She clapped her hands in unfeigned delight. "I've always wanted a gazebo. They're so romantic."

"I agree," he said, "though I've often wondered why we find them romantic. Is it conditioning? Years of old movies and TV commercials picturing love scenes in gazebos perched above scenic vistas?"

"Did you always try to analyze everything to death or did you learn that skill in law school?"

"I suspect it's a defense mechanism, acquired in childhood, God knows why."

As they approached the gazebo, several small white moths fluttered ahead of them, reminding Lia of the giant moth that had clung to her bedroom window. She hesitated.

"Want to go back?" Guy asked.

She'd never been afraid of moths. How foolish to let herself be put off by them. "No," she said, "I want to look at the gazebo."

Up close, the octagonal building seemed in fair shape, though its once-white paint had flaked off in patches and the exuberant green growth threatened to overwhelm it. When Guy forced aside the tangled vines obscuring the entrance, Lia saw that the three steps leading up to the gazebo appeared solid enough.

The conviction suddenly gripped her that she'd climbed these steps many times before, and that Guy had been with her then, as he was now. *Déjà vu*, wasn't that what the feeling was called?

"Shall we go up?" Guy's voice sounded oddly hoarse.

Anticipation tingled through her. Without answering, she set her foot on the first step. It creaked but held. She climbed the other two and found herself in an octagonal arbor of sweet-smelling greenery with the small yellow bells of Carolina jasmine all around her.

Guy took her hand and turned her to him. She could scarcely see his face in the darkness but it didn't matter. She knew so very well how he looked, how he tasted and how his body felt against hers. No other man had the same arousing scent of spice and male musk, no other man had the power to melt her bones with his touch. There could never be, would never be any other man for her.

He knew what he was doing was wrong but he had no choice. The sight, the scent, the touch of her drove him past the boundaries of reason and morality into the realms of madness where nothing mattered except possessing her. Each time they came together he swore it would be for the last time. It never was. She'd infiltrated his blood, she'd burrowed her way into his very soul.

He gripped her shoulders, his fingers digging into her soft, tempting flesh as he drew her against him. Was it love he felt for her? Sometimes the emotion seemed closer to hatred.

"Damn you," he growled as he lowered his head to taste the hot sweetness of her mouth, "I can't keep away."

Tasting her, kissing her, running his hands over the inviting curve of her hips inflamed him. Her eager, ardent response, her breathless little moans of passion aroused him past all reason. He tugged at her bodice until the fastenings gave way, cupping her white breasts in his hands, dipping his head to nibble at one nipple, then the other.

"Guy," she murmured. "Ah, Guy."

He raised his head in triumph, knowing she was as deeply and urgently aroused as he was. For the moment she was his love slave and would do anything he asked, anything at all. The most beautiful, most desirable woman in the parish and she was his, only his.

He'd take her here, on the floor of the gazebo, the perfume of jasmine mingling with her unforgettable woman's scent. He'd take her now.

Something soft fluttered against one of his cheeks, then the other, while at the same time something touched his forehead. He brushed his hand over his face, seeing a fluttering whiteness. Moths! Dozens of them. They'd invaded the gazebo. The damn things were getting in his hair, his ears.

Lia cried out, pulling free of him, making wordless noises of distress as she batted at the white moths flitting all around them both.

"They're even trying to get in my mouth!" Lia cried, so repelled by the moths brushing against her face that all she could think of was to escape from them. She groped blindly through the tangle of vines, searching for the way out.

When Guy parted the greenery, she stumbled down the steps and ran toward the house, aware he was keeping pace with her. When they reached the rear door, she glanced back and saw, to her dismay, a white cloud following them.

"Don't let them in!" she begged. "They're unnatural, horrible."

As though she'd been waiting, Sulie opened the door and they hurried inside. "Seems like some white magic got called up," Sulie said, gazing at the fluttering moths on the other side of the screen.

Lia brushed frantically at the few moths she found clinging to her opened shirt, flushing as she buttoned it, reminded of her abandoned behavior in the gazebo. The words Guy had used the day before, echoed in her mind—*Not me.*

Yet it *had* been her in his arms. Under her rebuttoned shirt her breasts still tingled from his caresses, just as her lips still burned from his kisses. It had happened so quickly. They'd barely set foot in the gazebo before she was caught in his wild embrace, as eager as he was to make love. But underlying her urgent passion had been the same sensation of wrongness that she'd felt when they kissed in the foyer yesterday.

A wrongness that he'd felt, too.

A moth fluttered past Lia and she shrank back. "Please get rid of them," she pleaded.

"Don't you worry," Sulie told her. "I be finding all them moths. They be just as good dead."

Lia didn't want to remain in the kitchen with the few moths that had gotten in, nor did she wish to go into one of the other rooms with Guy. She wasn't ready to face him until she'd tried to make some sense of what had happened.

"I know it's early," she said, without looking quite at him, "but I'm really tired. If you'll excuse me, I'm going up to bed."

Guy watched Lia leave the kitchen before turning to Sulie. "Do you get these plagues of moths often?" he asked.

She shook her head. "These ones be sent. For good, not bad. Maybe Ole Miss be reaching from beyond."

He realized Sulie was so steeped in superstition that there was no point in continuing the conversation. He couldn't believe as she did but there was no reason to insult her by saying so.

"Do you have any of that limeade left?" he asked. When she nodded, he said, "I'll take a glass of it up to my room with a couple of your ginger cookies, if I may."

In his bedroom, he set the tray Sulie had given him on the small table under Lafayette's picture. "General," he muttered, "I don't know what the hell's going on here."

He pulled off his shirt, flung it on a chair and, limeade in hand, crossed to the windows where he pushed apart the gold-trimmed curtains. Both windows were open but screened.

The dusk had deepened into full but not silent darkness. Frogs croaked their love songs from the bayou and somewhere a mockingbird sang. He stared into the night, smelling the faint scent of jasmine on the warm breeze. He knew he'd never again smell jasmine without remembering Lia.

He realized now that their passion in the gazebo had been as strange a coming together as what had happened in the foyer the day before, a strangeness that baffled him. He hadn't been in control either time and that alarmed him. When, exactly, had this strangeness begun? Not yesterday in the foyer, no. Before that. In his Oakland office, when Lia had walked through the door and he'd mistakenly thought he knew her.

To complicate matters, apart from this unnerving binding that drew them together, he wanted Lia. Not with the enforced urgency he'd felt in the foyer or the gazebo but with his own desire. If he could ever be certain any desire he had for Lia *was* his own. He was positive that if the moths hadn't distracted him, they'd have made love on the floor of the damn gazebo. He shook his head. That wasn't the right way, not the way he would choose. So maybe there was a difference.

Could he find a way to fight off whatever it was that took him over? To stay in control? To kiss Lia as Guy Russell and not as, not as—who? He smiled thinly. That was the question. How the hell was he supposed to find the answer? He didn't think much of his chances but, damn it, he meant to try.

Turning away from the window, he met Lafayette's commanding gaze. "So where do I start, sir?" he asked. The general had no answer. Guy shrugged.

Even if Lafayette had been able to reply no doubt it would be in French, a language he didn't know.

Perhaps he should have gone into that shop with the mandrake root in the window and bought an amulet to ward off the unknown. It might have proven to be more effective than his mother's advice for solving problems—a good night's sleep. He hadn't slept the night through since his arrival in New Orleans.

"For every problem, a solution exists," is what his father used to say when confronted with a complicated case. "Our task is to find that solution."

Guy shook his head. This time he would find no answers in law books. Sulie might provide a clue if he could persuade her to break what must have been a deathbed promise to Marie-Louise de la Roche. Even then, all Sulie might have to offer was more of her superstitious beliefs.

Whether or not it would help, he and Lia were overdue to hash over all that had happened since they met. Not tonight, though. She'd made that clear enough.

From the corner of his eye, he thought he caught a flutter of white but when he turned to look, the moth, if that's what it had been, was nowhere in sight. He scowled, annoyed with himself for being spooked by nothing.

Finish the drink, eat the cookies and go to bed, Russell, he advised himself. What else can you do?

Since the night was overwarm, he decided to sleep naked, leaving pajama bottoms within reach just in case. He turned out the light and lay on his back, listening to the chorus of frogs, both treble and bass, and hoping against hope he wouldn't dream. . . .

The mist drifted toward him from a long way off, a white mist that gradually took on a woman's form, lithe and graceful, a dark-haired woman whose face he couldn't see.

"Zha," she whispered when she neared him, *"Zha ray ve en."*

She paused, her face still turned from him, her white gown swirling around her. Then she raised her arm and beckoned to him to come to her. Unable to refuse, he took a step toward her. She began to drift away from him and he found himself compelled to follow where she led. As they came closer and closer to the waiting darkness, he fought to resist her spell, fearing what waited within that sinister gloom, sensing its evil.

His struggles were in vain. When she beckoned, he must follow where she led. The dark malevolence reached for her, enveloped all of her except for her beckoning hand.

No! I won't! he tried to shout, but he was powerless to speak, powerless to do anything but go to her. One step. Another. He knew the next step he took would be into hell itself. Fear curdled his gut, every cell in his body rebelled against that final step. . . .

With an incoherent cry, Guy woke to moonlit darkness. He lay without moving, his heart pounding, not sure where he was, not quite certain he *was* awake and all but positive that wherever he was, he wasn't alone.

A hand brushed his cheek. He flung himself back from the touch, at the same time striking out at whatever menaced him and hitting something soft.

"Oh!" The startled cry came from a woman.

Guy groped for the lamp next to the bed and switched it on. Lia, wearing the nightgown from the attic, stood beside his bed. She smiled at him, an alluring smile of invitation. Through the thin cotton of the gown, he could see the outline of her breasts, their nipples peaked in arousal.

For a brief instant he didn't move, staring at her with a longing that belonged to him alone, and then he was enveloped by a hot lust that rapidly escalated beyond his control. He reached for her, intent on tumbling her into his bed and ripping off the gown.

His hand closed over her arm. As she, obviously willing and eager, fell toward him, he saw something white in her black hair. A moth. Then she was in his arms, her lips seeking his. But he held back, aware without knowing why that he couldn't make love to her until the moth was destroyed. He fumbled through her hair to find the moth and pluck it out.

As he grasped the insect and squeezed it between his fingers, Lia shuddered and blinked. She stared at him, her eyes widening in startled dismay.

"What am I doing here?" she cried, leaning away from him. A moment later she slid from his bed and fled from the room.

Without pausing to clothe himself, Guy rushed after her. So she found it amusing to tease and then run away, did she? Not with him! He'd soon show her who had the last laugh. No one ever got the best of a ... A name trembled on the edge of his mind, eluding him and vanishing when he tried to grasp it.

He might have lost the name but Lia wouldn't escape him, he vowed as he saw the white flutter of her gown ahead and heard the creak of the attic door opening. Did she think she could fool him by hiding up there? She ought to realize by now that he was always the winner in the little games she was wont to play.

No, she couldn't fool him but he was a fool all the same. The truth was she had him in thrall. Try as he might he was unable to break free of her witch's spell. And it wasn't beyond the bounds of possibility she *was* a witch—de la Roche women had long possessed that reputation.

Whether she was witch or not, he was trapped by his unrelenting desire for her, a fiery need kindled anew each time he touched her.

He bounded up the attic stairs, making little noise with his bare feet, ignoring the darkness, certain she'd be visible in that sheer white gown, the one he'd given her himself. White was the color of purity and she was far from that but who wanted purity? Not he. At least not from her. He wanted her beneath him, hot and willing—nay, more than willing. Eager. Demanding everything he could give her and more.

He paused at the top of the stairs to scan the attic in the dim light slanting in through the small panes of the windows. Strange, he ought to be able to see the dark shapes of the many trunks and the discarded furniture that littered the floor but the place seemed oddly clear of such debris. He frowned, disoriented for a moment, on the verge of suspecting something was amiss.

A slight sound to his right caught his attention. He turned toward where there should be a wardrobe and with some relief saw its square outline. The door was open. Aha! She thought she was clever, did she? trying to secrete herself within the wardrobe.

He padded quietly over and peered around the open door, catching her in the act of removing the gown. Stepping around the wardrobe door, he grasped her, pulling her to him while she was still entangled in the gown.

She screamed, the sound muted by the folds of cloth covering her face.

"You must have known I'd find you, my love," he murmured as he worked the gown all the way off with one hand while holding her with the other. "You witch, I'd seek you out in hell itself." He tossed the gown aside and slid his hands caressingly over her soft curves, relishing the satiny feel of her skin.

She struggled to escape him, crying, "Let me go!"

He tightened his grip. "I'll never let you go."

"Guy," she pleaded, "please, listen. I wasn't myself there in your room. I don't even know how I got there. Or why I was wearing that gown."

Intent on making love to her, he ignored her words—little sense they made anyway—and bent his head to cover her mouth with his.

She turned her face from him, crying, "Guy! Don't do this."

Giving up the attempt to kiss her, he gripped her shoulders hard, holding her away from him. "What nonsense is this?" he growled.

"I'm trying to explain," she said. "It wasn't me. *She* took over."

He didn't understand. "She?"

"You know—the other. You've felt it, too. It's as though we're not Guy and Lia but some other man and woman."

"Lia?" he said, the name echoing ominously in his head, threatening to disorient him again. He shook his head to dispel the the sensation. "Who's Lia?"

She gasped. "You're not Guy!"

It must be some new game she expected him to play. Though he was in no mood for such silliness, he decided to humor her for the moment. "I certainly am Guy, my love. In the flesh, as you well know."

She was silent and, to his puzzlement, he felt her begin to tremble under his hands, almost as though she were actually afraid of him.

Finally she whispered, "If you don't believe I'm Lia, who do you think I am?"

He opened his mouth to tell her but the name on the tip of his tongue disappeared as a wave of realization washed over him. She *was* Lia. Not—not who? He couldn't remember; the other name was lost to him. He was vaguely aware that he'd pursued Lia to the attic and well aware that, though they were both naked, he was the only one aroused. She seemed more frightened than anything else. By him?

He let his hands drop from her shoulders. "What the hell happened?" he demanded.

She retreated and he heard the rustle of clothing. "Are you really yourself again?" she asked shakily.

Made uneasy by his own nakedness and still uncomfortably aroused, he said, "Can't we discuss this somewhere else?"

"I hope you're not suggesting we return to your bedroom." Now her voice held tartness.

"Name your neutral ground and I'll agree—once I get dressed."

Later, sitting across the kitchen table from Lia with the last of Sulie's limeade in his glass, Guy listened in dismay as she told him what he'd said and done in the attic.

"During all that went on you answered to your name, to Guy, and yet you didn't know I was Lia," she finished.

"Who did I think you were?"

"I don't know. When I asked, that seemed to bring you back to yourself."

"Didn't I call you anything at all?"

She hesitated, not meeting his gaze. "You—you called me your love."

He shook his head. "Nothing like this has ever happened to me before. I've never consciously called any woman 'my love.'"

"Well, *he* did."

Guy tried and failed to bring back any memory of his words or actions in the attic. The last thing he clearly remembered was waking from his nightmare to find Lia in his room.

"You were wearing that white nightgown from the attic wardrobe," he said, recalling how incredibly appealing she'd looked in the sheer gown.

Lia shifted in her chair. "I don't remember retrieving the gown and putting it on. And I didn't realize I was in your bed until I saw you killing that moth. I was really upset about finding myself there. All I could think of was getting away and putting the gown back in the wardrobe where it came from. That's why I went to the attic." Her gaze accused him. "I didn't know you meant to follow me."

"According to you, I didn't. *He* did. The he with my name."

"I wonder if someone named Guy used to live here. Do you suppose Sulie would know?"

He shrugged. "Sulie's a great one for keeping secrets. Even if she does know, she might not admit it."

Lia shivered. "It's scary being taken over like that."

"No argument." Guy glanced around the old-fashioned kitchen, observing the shadowed corners where the light from the ancient overhead fixture didn't penetrate. The whole damn house seemed to be full of secrets. He wasn't afraid but he *was* apprehensive. "I think you ought to leave this place."

She shook her head. "I'll be on guard." Eying him steadily, she added, "This strange attraction only happens when we're both here, doesn't it?"

"Not just here. Something occurred between us the moment we met. In Oakland, if you recall. Whatever the cause, I agree the bond's become increasingly potent since. Is that an effect of the house and grounds or would it be the same no matter where we were? I don't know. Still, if you want me to leave, I will. Even though I don't like you being alone in this place."

"I'm not alone. Sulie's with me."

"She's too old to be much protection. Besides, you can't be sure she can be trusted. Her loyalties seem tied to her dead employer."

Lia's expression grew stubborn. "This is my legacy. Something in the atmosphere of this house makes me believe I was meant to come here. I'm not leaving before the three months are up."

"Then I take it you want me to go."

She bit her lip. "No. You have to stay."

"*Have* to?" he echoed, wondering what she meant.

"Because it isn't right for you to leave. Not yet. Not before..." She paused, looking confused.

"Not before what?"

"I'm not certain. But I have this feeling it's important for the two of us to be here together."

"Reading the atmosphere again, are you?"

She shrugged. "Possibly. I do realize your time in New Orleans must be limited but—"

He waved his hand, cutting her off. "My time here's not the problem. *He* is. The other Guy. Apparently he's determined to make love to you no matter what, and, while I can control my behavior, we already know I sure as hell can't control his."

"I don't think it's me he wants," Lia said slowly. "It's the one who takes me over. The woman the white gown belongs to."

Guy stared at her. "For years I've seen that gown in my dreams, worn by the woman who beckons to me, the woman who looks like you. This situation grows more tangled by the minute and I don't like it. God only knows what may happen." He reached across the table and grasped her hand. "We can't stay here. Damn it, Lia, I refuse to be manipulated by anyone or anything. When we make love I want it to be us, to be you and me."

CHAPTER FIVE

The next morning, as though time-coordinated, Lia and Guy opened their bedroom doors at the same moment. They stared at each other across the hall, then broke into laughter.

"Two minds with but a single thought," she quipped as they walked toward the stairs.

"As long as they're *our* minds," he said. "How did you sleep?"

"Better than I expected to. How about you?"

"No dreams, at least none I recall."

"I think I heard a car drive up while I was getting dressed," she said. "Do you suppose Rebecca's paying another visit?"

"Not if Sulie's to be believed. I did hear the car, though, so someone must have come."

They found the visitor drinking coffee at the kitchen table while Sulie mixed pancake batter. He rose when they entered the kitchen and held out his hand.

"I'm Maurice Roche," he said, focusing on Lia. "My family dropped the rest of the name generations ago. May I call you Cousin Lia?"

She hesitated, eyeing the slim, bearded, thirtyish man who wore his dark hair long and bound back with a red bandanna. Before she'd decided what to say, Maurice grasped her hand and shook it.

"I would've brought my wife, but Dee won't come out here," he said before shifting his attention to Guy. "You must be the lawyer. I hope you've persuaded Cousin Lia to get shed of this old place as soon as she can."

"What makes you think Lia is your cousin?" Guy asked.

Maurice smiled. "Hell, we're both de la Roches, branch sinister, so we're bound to be some kind of cousins."

"So you're a bastard, too?" Lia said.

"Succinctly but truthfully put. I can only be grateful the old lady chose you instead of me. But I guess that was Rebecca's doing. She didn't want this place any more than I do."

"Are there any more of us?" Lia asked, deciding she rather liked her self-proclaimed cousin.

He shook his head. "Rebecca on one side, you and me on the other—that's it. Except that Dee's pregnant so there'll soon be a fourth."

Apparently Guy wasn't as ready to accept Maurice at face value as she was because, as the three of them sat down, she saw him eyeing her cousin dubiously.

"Did I hear you say you wouldn't have accepted the property if it had been left to you?" Guy asked him. At Maurice's nod, he added, "Why is that?"

"Everyone knows it's a bad place," Maurice told him. "I have enough problems without inheriting evil."

"Evil?" Lia echoed in surprise.

At the same time, Guy said, "That's a strong statement. Can you back it up with facts?"

Maurice took a deep draught from his coffee cup and set it down. "I can't put it into legalese but over the years more than one man has died on the grounds."

Remembering Sulie's warning, Lia said, "Were they bitten by poisonous snakes?"

"No more snakes here than any place else around," Maurice said. "The men, they drowned in the bayou. At night."

Lia glanced at Sulie and saw the old woman was nodding. "When she calls they got to come," Sulie muttered as she dropped pancake batter onto the sizzling griddle.

"Who?" Guy asked in a strange, tight voice. "Who is she and why do men have to come?"

"The Dread One, that's what they call her," Sulie said, turning to gaze directly at Guy. "Got *you* here, didn't she?"

Thinking of Guy's recurring dream of a woman in a white gown, a frisson of fear trickled along Lia's spine. Stop it, she admonished herself. The Dread One can't be more than an old Louisiana superstition. How can some bayou legend have anything to do with Guy?

"There's supposed to be a hidden grave somewhere on the property near the bayou," Maurice said. "Hers, that's what they say."

"Does this Dread One have a name?" Lia demanded.

Maurice shrugged. "I never heard a name mentioned. My grandfather used to say that way back the de la Roche family fled France for Louisiana because an ancestor's wife was in danger of being burned as a witch. Maybe it's the witch's grave."

From the corner of her eye, Lia noticed Sulie shaking her head. She turned to confront the old woman, asking, "Do you know?"

"Best not to talk about the Dread One," Sulie muttered. "Ole Miss don't like it."

"Ole Miss to Sulie," Maurice said, "Aunt Marie-Louise to Rebecca, Miss de la Roche to me." He fixed his gaze on Lia. "What you need to keep in mind about Rebecca is that she never did anyone a favor in her life. If she talked the old lady into willing you the property, you can be sure Rebecca must benefit in some way and that you won't. My advice is to chuck the old place, Cuz, and get out of here before it's too late."

"Let's get one thing straight, Maurice," Guy said as Sulie set a platter of steaming hot pancakes on the table in front of him. "Is it a documented fact that there was an illegitimate branch of the de la Roche family?"

"Hey, it wasn't that uncommon in New Orleans in the old days. Having two families was the custom and our de la Roche ancestor was no exception. It happened so long ago that it doesn't matter anymore. Except to Rebecca, of course. She's never acknowledged me as a blood relative."

"But Rebecca told me she'd persuaded Aunt Marie-Louise to recognize me as a true de la Roche," Lia protested.

"You can believe that if you want. I don't." Maurice's voice held a tinge of anger. "Rebecca never had an altruistic thought in her life."

"Getting back to the bar sinister hanging over some of the de la Roches," Guy said. "Are there family records?"

"Sulie said Aunt Marie-Louise burned her papers before she died," Lia reminded him. "Does it really make any difference in my inheriting the property?"

"I don't think so. But just in case there's any question, I'd like to see some proof of the two-family business. Lawyers worry about this kind of thing."

"Why?" Maurice asked. "Who's going to sue? I don't want any part of it and neither does Rebecca. If she did, you can be sure she wouldn't have been so eager for Cousin Lia to inherit."

"I wouldn't like to see the will hung up in probate on a technicality," Guy said. "Lia wants everything settled as soon as possible."

"Be a chestful of papers in the library," Sulie put in unexpectedly. "Ole Miss don't burn those. Dream tell her not to."

Had Guy's lady in white appeared in Marie-Louise's dream, too? Lia wondered, and then dismissed the thought as fanciful. "Help yourself to the pancakes," she said to Maurice.

He rose. "Thanks, but I'd best be on my way. Dee'll be beside herself if I stay any longer. She didn't like me coming here and I can't say I blame her." He shifted his shoulders uneasily. "Even in daylight you can feel the wrongness. I wouldn't stay here at night for any amount of money. And neither should you, Cuz. Or your lawyer friend." He glanced at Sulie. "I guess you're safe here after all these years."

"Be safe enough," Sulie said. "Me, I don't be letting no one hurt Miss Lia."

"I hope I'll see you again," Lia told Maurice. "It's great to find relatives when you thought you had none."

"I can see you're not going to take my advice," he said as he gripped her hand in farewell. "Promise me you'll at least think it over."

She nodded, though she knew nothing he'd said could make her change her mind. Wrongness? Evil? She didn't feel either of those things here. The house had welcomed her. And the strange attraction between her and Guy might have nothing whatsoever to do with this property. *Her* property. The sense they'd met before had first happened in Oakland, not in New

Orleans. So the disturbing force that drew them together couldn't be emanating from her house.

As for Guy's recurring dreams, since they'd begun in his childhood in Oakland he could hardly connect them to the de la Roche estate. And while he may have thought the dream woman resembled her, he hadn't been too sure and one long white nightgown looks much like any other.

About Maurice—she'd been inclined to trust him, but should she? What if he had some hidden reason to want her to give up her inheritance?

"That one, he change his name but he can't be changing his looks," Sulie said. "He be a de la Roche, no mistake. Even Ole Miss say so."

"I noticed a resemblance between you and Maurice," Guy told Lia. "I don't doubt the relationship. What bothers me is the legitimacy angle. I'd like to take a look at those papers, Sulie. Where exactly is the chest?"

Once they'd finished breakfast, Sulie led the way to the library where, while they gaped in amazement, she pushed a hidden lever that opened a section of what had appeared to be no more than a paneled wall under built-in bookcases.

Guy knelt, grasped the metal handle of a brass chest the size of a footlocker and pulled it free of the recess. "Any more secret compartments you'd like to tell us about?" he asked Sulie.

"This be the onliest one Ole Miss show me."

"I'm surprised she didn't swear you to secrecy about this the way she did everything else."

Sulie shrugged. "Must be she wanted you to find it." Without another word, she turned and left the room.

The lid of the chest, engraved with *fleur-de-lis*, raised easily, revealing various ledgers and an oblong, elaborately decorated enameled box. Guy lifted out the top ledger and, while he examined what was inside, Lia removed the box.

"Oh!" she exclaimed when she opened it and gazed down at glittering green gems set into gold. "Can these actually be emeralds?"

Guy set aside the ledger to look at her find. "I suspect you've uncovered the family jewels," he said.

They sorted through the jewelry, discovering all the stones were green. "If they *are* emeralds," Guy said, "that box contains a small fortune."

Lia, struggling to open the compartment of a gold brooch that held a large emerald, couldn't quite believe the gems were real. "I've heard emeralds are unlucky if the wrong person wears them," she said.

As she spoke, the brooch sprang open to reveal a wisp of hair. Speechless, she stared from the hair to Guy and back.

"What's the matter?" he asked.

In answer, she offered him the brooch and he took it from her. "A lock of hair," he said uncomprehendingly.

"Auburn hair," she pointed out. "Hair the same color as yours."

Guy looked closer at the open compartment of the brooch. "Quite a coincidence."

Yes, of course, it had to be a coincidence, Lia told herself.

"I've heard women used to put hair from their babies in lockets and brooches," he said, "but this hair isn't fine enough to be a child's."

"It's from her lover's head." Lia spoke without thinking, the words coming from somewhere outside her. "He angered her when he wouldn't accept a lock of her hair in return."

She drew in her breath when she realized what she'd said, all the more upset because she knew deep in her heart that she'd spoken the truth.

Guy snapped the brooch shut, the click seeming to echo ominously in the room.

"I know." He spoke as though the words were wrenched from his throat. "Just as I know he loved her and hated her at the same time."

They stared at each other, waiting apprehensively for what would happen next until the shrill ring of the phone in the entry broke the spell. Lia sprang to her feet and ran from the room. She caught the phone on the third ring.

"May I speak to Guy Russell?" a man's voice said.

After calling Guy to the phone she couldn't make herself return to the library alone so she headed for the kitchen in search of Sulie. When she found her, Lia insisted on helping by cutting up the vegetables for the Creole dish Sulie was preparing.

She finished the vegetables, time passed and Guy didn't appear. Since his call wasn't likely to have lasted this long, she decided he must have returned to the library. Somewhat ashamed of having run off like a frightened child, she went back to find him.

She found him sitting at the desk with an open ledger in front of him. The brass chest was closed and there was no sign of the jewelry box. He glanced up as she entered.

"I've found what I was looking for," he said. "One Phillipe de la Roche, the progenitor of the two branches, took the trouble to diagram a separate family tree for each branch." He grimaced. "Rebecca and Maurice are right—your side is illegitimate. I'll have to consult with DuBois about this when he returns from Europe."

"But he already knows I come from the wrong side," she protested.

"I still want to talk to him. Lawyers like all *i*'s dotted and all *t*'s crossed. And I have another reason as well. My own reason." Guy took a deep breath. "The man who called me is named Lafitte. He's a local private investigator I hired to search for my parents. He hasn't made any progress toward finding my mother but he did turn up what may be a clue to my father."

Guy paused. "Do you remember DuBois calling me Mr. Revenir when we walked into his office?"

Lia nodded.

"I told Lafitte about it and apparently DuBois wasn't far off. Lafitte says his investigations have turned up photos that could have been of me. I bear a striking likeness to some of the members of the Revenir family, besides having their same eye and hair color."

From the moment they'd met, Lia had found his combination of amber eyes and auburn hair unusual as well as attractive. "Will you be meeting the Revenirs?" she asked.

He shook his head. "Unfortunately Lafitte couldn't turn up a single live Revenir. A woman who'd known the last of them told him the line was cursed, that all the Revenirs died young." His voice was bleak and her heart went out to him. How frustrating to uncover a part of your origins only to find no one in the family alive.

Crossing to the desk, she reached to give him a comforting pat, then held, suddenly cautious, afraid of what might happen if she touched him.

He noticed her hesitation and smiled wryly.

"Me, I knew you for a Revenir when you walked into this place." Sulie spoke from the open doorway, startling them both. "Knew sooner or later she'd find one of you. Evil be coming sure as sundown. Trouble is, Miss Lia be caught in the trap right along with you, Revenir man. Gonna take more than Ole Miss reaching from beyond to save her." Sulie advanced into the room. "I can help some, Miss Lia, but it look like you got to try to save yourself."

"I don't understand," Lia said. "You'll have to explain what you mean. What does Guy have to do with this place?"

"He be a Revenir. And you be a de la Roche. Means you got powers like Ole Miss had."

Lia shook her head. "I don't have any so-called powers, Sulie."

"If you'd start at the beginning we'd have a better chance of understanding," Guy said. From the tautness of his voice, Lia realized he was hanging on to his patience with difficulty.

Sulie shot him a dark look. "You bring trouble here, Revenir man, that's what. Stir up evil. Evil gonna reach out for you. Miss Lia, she be in evil's path." Sulie shook her head. "Miss Lia, you got to be putting your trust in the snakes, lest darkness take you both."

"Snakes!" Lia cried. "Whatever are you talking about?"

"Some say voodoo 'cause the power come to you from fire and snakes."

Lia moved closer to Guy, frightened not so much by Sulie's words as she was by the alarming surge within her, a wild and feral urge awakened by what the old woman had said about power, about her having powers. What was happening to her?

Sulie peered at her and nodded. "Be there, like I say. Can't hide voodoo power no more than a Revenir can hide fire hair and yellow-flame eyes."

Lia shivered and Guy put his arm around her. Sulie cast her eyes heavenward. "Be asking for trouble, you two, that's what." Shaking her head, she turned from them and left the library.

Did Sulie know what could occur when she and Guy touched? Lia wondered. Would it happen now? Would they be consumed by a lust that wasn't theirs alone? She ought to move away from him but she desperately needed the comfort of his arms.

He held her lightly, tenderly, his hand stroking her back as he murmured words she wanted to believe. "It's all right, don't be upset, it's all right."

But it wasn't all right. Though she'd insisted to Maurice earlier that the house welcomed her, Sulie's warning had brought menace into the atmosphere. She stirred in Guy's embrace, pulling free to look up at him.

"You've got to remember that Sulie is an old woman," he said. "Either her mind is slipping or she's so steeped in superstition that she has a twisted view of the world. Don't let what she says disturb you."

"It's not just Sulie," Lia said. "She had nothing to do with the auburn hair inside that old brooch—hair that could have come from the head of one of your Revenir ancestors. It might mean a Revenir was involved with a de la Roche."

"A Revenir named Guy? Is that what you're suggesting?"

"You have to admit it's a possibility."

Guy frowned. "A possibility, no more than that."

"But if it's true, that could explain why—" She broke off as she realized the implications of what she was about to say. Did she, who had never believed in ghosts, really think some kind of Revenir spirit haunted the mansion, a spirit able to assume control of Guy?

And even if true, how did that explain their mutual bonding in Oakland?

"The best solution is for us both to leave here, leave New Orleans altogether and return to California," he said.

She couldn't deny it. Yet at the same time she felt bound to the house in a way she couldn't explain. "I was drawn here for a purpose," she told him, searching for the right words.

He nodded. "Even before Maurice warned us Rebecca wasn't to be trusted, I couldn't quite swallow her version of why Marie-Louise de la Roche left the estate to you. If the old woman truly wished to make amends to the so-called wrong branch of the family, why not divide the estate between you and Maurice? Why just you? What's behind it? I'm becoming more and more convinced you were deliberately maneuvered here for reasons I don't understand. Or like."

"And so were you."

Guy blinked. "Why do you say that? I made arrangements to come to New Orleans before you and I ever met."

"Maybe so, but we *did* meet and here you are at the de la Roche mansion, a place you never would have known existed if you hadn't met me. Furthermore, Sulie recognized you on sight as a Revenir."

"Or says she did. Don't forget she could have been standing at the library door long enough to hear me tell you about Lafitte's findings."

"She knew who you were when you walked in the front door of this house for the first time. Don't you recall how odd she acted?"

Guy scowled. "I don't want to believe any of this. I've always mistrusted the intangible. Like those infernal childhood dreams. If I stretched a point or two, I could connect them with you and with this place like some sort of an early-warning signal."

"Maybe they were. Maybe they still *are* a warning. Maybe deep in your heart you know it and that's why you're anxious to leave here."

"What I really want is for you to leave with me." He reached for her hand, holding it between both of his. "I don't want you to come to any harm."

Though he held only her hand, she felt as though he'd embraced her totally, keeping her safe and secure. For a long moment she relished the comforting sensation. If only they could be left alone to find their own way to each other and not be forced into an overwhelming intimacy that didn't belong to them. Would that be possible if they ran away from the shadowy menace of this place and returned to California? Even as she wondered, something inside told her that no matter how hard she tried, she wasn't yet powerful enough to break the invisible ties that bound her here. At the same time she felt her infant powers flutter within as if impatient to be born, strange and frightening but also exhilarating.

Lia pulled her hand free of Guy's. "I can't leave until whatever brought me here lets me go."

"That's nonsense!"

She shook her head, keeping what she felt within her a secret, certain of Guy's disbelief. *Snakes,* she thought, and this time she didn't shudder. *Snakes and fire.*

CHAPTER SIX

Lia lay in her bed, gazing at the moonlight slanting in through her open curtains and wistfully wishing Guy was beside her. Her Guy, not the frightening other. But how could she ever be certain one wouldn't change into the other? She couldn't even be sure she wouldn't be taken over herself by whatever invisible force haunted the place.

Guy had urged that they flee from the unseen menace—but could they? Sulie seemed absolutely certain Guy would find it impossible to leave the estate. Lia sighed. Whether Sulie was right or not made little difference. Guy was determined to take her away with him if he did leave. And she wasn't going.

Not because the estate was hers. She knew now it could never truly belong to her nor would she be able to feel at home here. Someone—*something*—else was mistress here. Perhaps that was why Rebecca hadn't wanted any part of the estate and why both she and Maurice were afraid to come to the house. Lia couldn't blame them but she was damned if she was going to be driven away without a fight.

Marie-Louise had lived in the mansion all her life without any harm coming to her. Was it because, as

Sulie insisted, Ole Miss had some kind of power that kept evil at bay?

Sulie said Lia had power, too. Was it true? Lia closed her eyes, searching inside herself for what she'd sensed before but failed to find it. She felt alone and vulnerable and unsure of her decision to stay. She thought of getting up and going downstairs to call her grandparents and be reassured by their familiar voices but she rejected the idea. What could she say? They hadn't wanted her to come to New Orleans in the first place and she couldn't bear to trouble them with her anxieties.

There was Sulie, who would listen to her and maybe understand. Sulie, though, with her predictions of trouble ahead, wasn't likely to be any comfort.

That left Guy, the one person she really wanted to be with. Lia sat up. Why shouldn't she take a chance and go to him? She slid from her bed and reached the door before she paused to reconsider. What was she doing? It was far too risky to enter his bedroom. God knows which Guy she would find there.

With a resigned sigh, she retraced her steps, flipped on the bedside lamp, crawled into bed and picked up one of her paperbacks. After rereading the first page three times and then not taking in what she'd read, she gave it up as futile and dropped the book back onto the old-fashioned nightstand. Thinking maybe one of the old volumes on the shelves underneath might hold her interest, she reached for one at random and settled back.

The book fell open by itself somewhere near the middle and she found herself gazing at a drawing of a nude woman dancing around a fire, so entangled in the coils of a gigantic snake that it wasn't clear which was snake and which was woman. For a long moment Lia stared in fascinated horror before slamming the book shut and thrusting it quickly back on the shelf.

But she couldn't rid herself of the image. When she finally shut off the light and started to drift off, a voice whispered, *You need the snakes. Don't fear them, trust them. Kos waits for you.*

Lia half roused, uncertain if she was dreaming, the name echoing in her mind—*Kos, Kos, Kos . . .*

Guy rose early, discovering Lia wasn't up yet. After downing coffee and a cinnamon roll in the kitchen, he let himself out the back door into the warm morning for a walk. Though he recalled no dreams, he'd slept poorly, disturbed by the fear he and Lia were on a perilous one-way street with danger ahead and no hope of returning.

He ought to be able to come up with a plan but he seemed to have lost his ability to reason logically. Those colleagues who'd hailed him as a first-class analytical thinker wouldn't know what to make of him now.

It was as if the heat and humidity combined with his surroundings to create a miasma that sapped his will and clouded his mind in the same way as the encroaching growth threatened to destroy the gazebo he was passing.

The predatory greenery had taken over the grounds, creating a jungle. Maurice had mentioned a hidden grave but if there *was* a grave on the property it would be all but impossible to find in this tangled growth. Always assuming anyone would want to find a witch's grave. If that's who was buried there. And if he believed in witches.

Damn, he wasn't thinking straight. What he needed to do, Guy decided, was drive into the city to get away from this place for a few hours. First he'd visit Lafitte to see if anything new about his birth parents had turned up. Then he'd stop at DuBois, Labranche and Charters. DuBois wouldn't be there but Bob LaBranche might be able to arrange for Lia to hire a gardener and charge the estate.

Should he ask Lia to come into the city with him? He shook his head. She'd be safe enough here during the daylight hours and he really needed to be alone. He might be able to think more clearly if she wasn't with him.

What were these forces from the past that threatened them? He needed information, needed to learn more about the de la Roches so he and Lia would have some idea of what they were up against. Maurice didn't know enough to be of help and Sulie was too closemouthed. Rebecca? Maybe. She ought to know de la Roche family history and, if he visited her, she might be willing to talk to him about the past. She was worth a try, certainly. There *had* to be a solution and he might learn enough to come up with one.

When he returned to the house Lia was still upstairs, presumably sleeping, so he asked Sulie to tell her that he'd gone into New Orleans but would be back before dark.

"I don't think so," Sulie said, her words stopping him at the door.

Controlling his exasperation—why must she be so cryptic?—he tried for clarification. "Are you saying you won't tell her?"

"Won't be needing to. You ain't going 'cause you can't."

Refusing to argue with her since he knew it would be useless, he exited, got into his rental car, rammed the key into the ignition and turned it. Nothing happened. He removed the key, checked to make sure it was the right one and tried again. Then again. Still nothing.

"Damn," he muttered, "the battery must be dead."

Either Marie-Louise had never owned a car or had sold it before she died because there was no other vehicle on the estate. It was this car or nothing. Grumbling, he returned to the house.

"Any gas stations or garages near here?" he asked Sulie, half expecting her to say she'd told him he wasn't going anyplace.

"Be Cajun Joe's down the road a piece," she said without so much as glancing at him.

He found the garage listed in the telephone book and called.

"Be there in about fifteen minutes or so," Joe told him.

It was closer to a half hour before the tow truck pulled up next to Guy's car. Joe jumped down from the cab and asked for the key. "I always try to start 'em before I mess around," he said. "You just never know."

To Guy's annoyance and embarrassment, the car started the moment Joe turned the key in the ignition.

"Happens sometimes," Joe said consolingly as he proceeded to turn off the motor and restart the car several times with no difficulty. "Don't seem to be any problem with the battery now but I'll leave her running just in case," he added as he got out.

Guy paid him for the trip he'd made, then watched the tow truck drive away while beside him the rental car motor purred sweetly. Getting in, he backed the car out carefully, taking no chances on stalling it when he shifted gears to go forward. Everything went well until he reached the estate gates. There, between the griffins gazing stonily into the distance, the car stopped dead and, no matter what Guy tried, refused to start again.

He got out, slammed the door and cursed. What the hell was he supposed to do now? Call Cajun Joe back? No, damn it, he'd phone the rental car people and insist they exchange this lemon for one that ran. Leaving the keys in the car, he marched back to the house, fuming.

He said not a word to Sulie as he hurried through the kitchen on his way to the phone in the entry. He was searching through the yellow pages when he heard a motor. Could be the truck that picked up the laundry but he thought it sounded more like a car. Putting the phone book aside, he went to see who it was.

Rebecca de la Roche was just emerging from her sports car when he opened the kitchen door. "Who the devil left that car smack in the middle of the entrance?" she demanded. "I had to climb into the thing and drive it out of the way before I could get my car past."

"You were able to drive that car?" he asked in surprise.

"What else could I do?" she said testily.

"The car started all right?"

"Of course." She spoke as though she couldn't imagine any car not starting for her.

"I had some trouble with it," he admitted. Turning to usher Rebecca into the house, he noticed Sulie watching them through the screen. No doubt gloating because her prophecy seemed to be fulfilled, he thought with considerable irritation.

"I was planning to visit you," he told Rebecca.

She flashed him a coquettish smile, apparently no longer annoyed. "How exciting. That is, unless you'd planned to bore me with tedious legal details."

Sulie retreated, allowing them to enter the kitchen. "We'll have ice tea in the morning room," Rebecca told the old woman who gazed at her blank faced while saying nothing.

Rebecca chose the wicker divan to sit on, gazing up at him in invitation. Instead of sitting next to her, Guy seated himself in a nearby chair. She shrugged. "I keep forgetting the house has no air-conditioning, making it much too warm for us to indulge in a *tête-à-tête*. Besides, Cousin Lia might object, *n'est-ce pas?*"

"I'm afraid I don't speak French," Guy said, deliberately avoiding any mention of Lia.

"What a shame. We New Orleanians know French is truly the language of romance."

"Speaking of romance," he said, "we found what appears to be a heirloom brooch. When Lia opened its compartment she found a lock of hair—from some long-ago lover's head, she believes. Do you happen to remember any romantic tales about de la Roche ancestors?"

Rebecca pulled a folding fan from her bag, unfurled it and waved the fan gently in front of her face. "Is romance really the right word for what you seek? Aunt Marie-Louise occasionally hinted at ancient family scandals but she was old-fashioned enough to keep whatever she knew a secret."

"A Revenir may have been involved with one of the de la Roches," he persisted. "Have you ever heard that name?"

"Since the Revenirs were an old New Orleans family, naturally I know of them. I believe Tanguay Revenir was the last of the line and he died some years ago. I don't know about his ancestors but he was reputed to be a hell-raiser, especially with the ladies. Come to think of it, he had auburn hair something like yours." The smugness in her smile made Guy wonder if she'd suspected all along that he was in some way related to the Revenirs.

While he was forming his next question, she said, "I understand Maurice Roche came to see Cousin Lia. I do hope she didn't encourage the man. He's one of those would-be musicians with minimal talent who are always looking for a handout."

"We did meet Maurice."

"Actually, that's why I'm here. As I've mentioned before, I don't care for this old place but I felt I had to warn Cousin Lia that he'll sponge off her as much as he can. I refuse to give him even the time of day. Where is Lia, by the way? I do hope she's not ill."

"I believe she's still asleep."

Rebecca raised her eyebrows. "Keeping her up late, are you?" She reached over and tapped his knee with her fan. "Naughty, naughty. Especially since you'll be returning to California all too soon and leaving poor, dear Lia behind to pine."

"It's nothing like that," he said shortly, annoyed at her insinuations and at himself for reacting to them.

"I think the man protests too much. We may have a true case of *rêve à deux* here. Ah, *très* romantic."

He clenched his jaw to prevent himself from responding. She knew he didn't understand French and she was using not only snide remarks about his relationship with Lia but also his ignorance of the language to try to prod him into some sort of indiscreet outburst. Why? What did she expect him to reveal?

He no longer believed Rebecca had come to warn them about Maurice; he couldn't even be sure that what she said about the man was true. She was here for information of some kind. What could it be? Had she been anticipating trouble? Expecting something to happen to Lia? Guy tensed at the thought. Damn the woman!

"Do you have any particular reason for asking if Lia might be ill?" he asked.

Rebecca leaned forward. "Is she?"

Two could play at the answer a question with a question game. "Did you expect her to be?"

Rebecca sat back and began fanning herself again. "What an odd thing to ask. No one expects a person to be ill."

"I thought maybe you were aware of something unhealthy about this place."

"Aunt Marie-Louise lived to a great age here," Rebecca pointed out.

"Yet you seem to shun the estate."

"My taste has never run to decaying out-of-the-way properties. Really, counselor, I'm getting the distinct impression you're treating me as a hostile witness."

"I'm merely trying to do all I can to make certain Lia will be safe here."

She sighed. "Can it be said a woman is truly safe anywhere in the world today?"

"I think there may be a few spots left," he said dryly.

"Considering the thrust of your questions, you obviously don't believe this is one of the safe spots. So I assume you've been listening to Maurice. You can't trust a word the man says."

"I found it interesting that evil was one of the words he used."

Guy expected a quick rebuttal but instead Rebecca lapsed into silence. "If he used that word," she said at last, "then he must have told you the *rusalka* story. I knew someone would sooner or later. That tale scared me to death when I was a child, but, of course, it's only backcountry superstition."

The odd word meant nothing to Guy. *"Rusalka?"*

"A Russian friend of mine who heard the bayou legend told me that in Russian myth a *rusalka* is a dreadful female spirit who lures men into rivers and streams and drowns them. I've borrowed his word because it fits."

"You prefer it to the Dread One?"

Rebecca dropped her fan and covered her ears with her hands the way a child would. "No! Don't say it!"

It was the first honest reaction he'd seen from her. Almost immediately she recovered, picked up the fan and put it into her bag. She glanced at her watch and rose. "I really must be going. Do tell Lia I'm sorry to have missed her."

Getting to his feet, Guy said, "I'll do that. But I have a favor to ask. Since I can't trust my rental car, if you're returning to the city, I'd like a ride into—"

She cut him off. "Oh, but I'm not. I have an appointment in Baton Rouge and I'm on my way there. Otherwise I'd be happy to give you a lift. Sorry."

He wasn't sure he believed her but he nodded politely. After she left he went out and tried his car again but whatever magic Rebecca had used on it had vanished because the car wouldn't start for him.

"The hell with it," he muttered. "I'll call Lafitte instead of driving into town."

When he reached the private investigator's office, Lafitte wasn't encouraging. "I'm afraid what you've given me on your mother is too tenuous to be useful," he said. "The locket is of a type sold across the country, so I can't narrow down where it might have been purchased and the cutout photo inside isn't helpful because there's no indication where it was taken. It's no good me tramping the streets asking random strangers if they've ever seen this woman before and that's about all there's left to do."

Guy swallowed his disappointment, letting himself recognize that it would take a miracle for anyone to identify a nameless woman from a small, rather blurred cutout of her face. "At least I have an idea who my father might have been," he said.

"You understand there's no proof," Lafitte said, "but after seeing those pictures I'd bet on him being a Revenir. When you stop by the office I'll return the locket and give you copies of the Revenir photos, too."

"I'd appreciate that. By the way, did the woman you talked to tell you the first name of the Revenir she knew—the last one to die?"

"Yeah. Tanguay, she said. Come to think of it, the name's usually shortened. To Guy. Could be another link." Lafitte sounded pleased.

Guy smiled. No actual proof but a marked probability. He thanked the P.I. and hung up just as Lia came down the stairs.

"I overslept," she said, "and I'm starved."

Standing at the foot of the staircase, he gazed up at her, struck anew by her beauty, hoping the warmth in her brown eyes was for him. He not only wanted her but felt an urgent need to protect her, to keep her safe from any kind of harm.

She smiled and he resisted the impulse to take her into his arms. "Sleepyhead," he accused.

As they walked toward the kitchen, he told her about the balky rental car. "Until I call and have the agency bring out another," he said as they entered the kitchen, "I guess we're more or less stranded here."

"Won't do no good to get another car," Sulie advised, overhearing. "No way you can leave this place lest she lets you go and she ain't gonna do that, Revenir man. She got you here and she gonna keep you here."

"I'll give it a shot, anyway," he said, having decided to humor Sulie.

"You be telling Miss Lia who was here this morning?" Sulie asked. Without waiting for him to answer, she went on. "That Miss Rebecca, she act like she own the place, ordering me around. I don't be working for her, never did and never will."

Her outburst made Guy realize Sulie hadn't bothered to bring the ice tea Rebecca had ordered and he smiled at the old woman. He might get annoyed because she was so superstitious and secretive, but he truly admired her character.

"I thought Rebecca didn't like the house," Lia said. "What brought her here?"

Sulie spoke before Guy could. "Said a pack of nonsense 'bout Maurice and wanted to know was you ailing. Did maybe get something right, though. Told him—" she jerked her head toward Guy "—that you and he was *rêve à deux.*"

So Sulie had been eavesdropping. It seemed to be a habit of hers.

Lia shook her head. "That sounds like French. What does it mean?"

"Just like him, you don't know French?" Sulie asked. "Too bad. Ain't no good way to say it in English. You both be together in some kind of dream, only you both be awake, can't put it no plainer."

Lia and Guy exchanged glances and he saw his own surprise mirrored in her eyes. Sulie's definition came close to what had happened to them. But how had Rebecca known? Or Sulie, for that matter.

He repeated the French phrase, his pronunciation making Sulie frown. "Don't sound right. You listen to me." She spoke slowly, drawing out the words until they sounded strangely familiar. Yet he'd never before heard the phrase until today.

"*Ray ve,*" he echoed, and suddenly froze, recognizing some of the nonsense words from his dream. "*Zha,*" he muttered. "*Zha ray ve en.*"

"No, no," Sulie chided, "you be saying different words. *Je reviens* mean something else. What it mean be 'I come back.'"

The hair rose on Guy's nape. *I come back.* Those were the words the woman in his dreams had been saying to him all these years. Telling him in French she'd come back. To him? For him? But how could that be? And yet—maybe she had come back. Through Lia. But who was she? And why did she haunt his dreams?

Lia touched his shoulder, making him jump. "Guy? Are you all right?"

He shook his head. "I'm drowning in illogic." He dredged up a smile. "Go ahead and eat, I'm going to make a few phone calls."

The line to the rental car agency was busy. He reached the law firm and spoke to Bob LaBranche who promised to take care of finding a gardener on estate money. When Guy still couldn't get through to the rental agency, he lost patience and left the house by the front door.

The car, parked just off the drive by the entrance, still wouldn't start—not that he'd expected it to. He got out and stood between the griffins in the heat of midday, sweat trickling from what seemed like every pore. Turning to face the house, he muttered, "Damn you, whoever you are. If you think you can outsmart a Russell, you're—"

Guy stopped abruptly. He wasn't a Russell except by adoption. But he might well be a Revenir by birth. And that made a difference.

"No!" The word spewed from him. Russell or Revenir, nothing was going to stop him from leaving the estate grounds, even if he had to walk.

Setting his jaw, he faced forward and began to march determinedly through the driveway entrance. He'd taken no more than two steps before a feeling of intense dread settled over him like a shroud. He knew beyond any shadow of a doubt that if he left the estate something terrible would happen to Lia.

CHAPTER SEVEN

As Lia sipped her coffee in the kitchen, she heard Guy open and shut the front door and she wondered where he was going. Glancing at Sulie, she blinked when she met the old woman's intent gaze. All thoughts of Guy fled as Sulie's bright, black eyes seemed to stare into her very soul.

Before Lia could force herself to break the contact, she felt power beginning to coil inside her, urging her to begin, to gather the forces she needed before it was too late. *Go to the bayou,* a voice whispered in her mind. *Go there and call them to you.*

"Ole Miss, she be on your side," Sulie said. "You listen to what she tell you."

Was it Ole Miss she'd heard whispering to her last night? Lia wondered. No conscious decision drove her to her feet and through the back door, she felt compelled to do as the voice ordered. Purpose and knowledge flowed into her as she followed a barely perceptible path though the wild, proliferating growth at the rear of the house.

Call, yes, she would call and they would hear. They would hear and obey and, when they came, her power would be set free. She knew now why she'd been named Ophelia for the name meant she had control over all the ophidians. All snakes. When she called them, they would come to her and do her bidding.

They twined through her mind, some dark as midnight, others glowing with jeweled colors, some no bigger around than her forefinger, others as thick as a man's thigh, all sleek and beautiful, all hers.

They waited for her at the bayou, some on land, some in the dark bayou water. They'd been waiting since her arrival, waiting for her call, waiting to help her release and refine her power. Why had she ever feared snakes when they were hers to command? There was but little time left. Why had she delayed so long?

She passed between two ancient magnolia trees whose branches met in a canopy above her head, going on until she reached a small clearing near the bayou. Though heavy growth between her and the water hid it from her view, she breathed in the smell of the bayou, heavy and dark. Pausing in the clearing's circular center, a place where nothing, not even a weed grew, she began to hum, soft and low. A hot and humid breeze sprang up, carrying her humming along the low bayou banks and over the water.

They came, as she knew they would, slithering swiftly through the greenery, stopping when they reached the circle of bare ground as though it formed an invisible barrier between them and her. Forked tongues flicking to taste her scent on the air, they coiled to watch her. Still humming, the faint musk of the snakes in her nostrils, she turned sunwise, the way of the light, to view each and every one, and, as she turned, power thrust up from deep inside her, vibrating through every pore as she absorbed their silent offering.

When she completed the circle, she must choose. One snake and one only would be hers to keep for as long as she had need but the concerted strength of all would be contained within her choice. The gem-bright colors of one tempted her. A vivid green snake swayed so hypnotically she was almost confused into picking him. Then her gaze fell on a blacksnake nearly as thick as her arm. She recalled the woman with the snake in the book in her bedroom and she understood the picture had been an omen.

Raising her arms straight out in front of her, she extended her left and right forefingers, holding them side by side as she pointed at the blacksnake. "My friend, my colleague," she whispered, "join me. Help me. Be my guide."

The blacksnake uncoiled and slithered past the invisible barrier, gliding across the bare ground toward her. As though that were a signal, the rest of the snakes left the clearing to vanish in the overgrowth.

When the blacksnake reached her, she bent and gathered his five-foot length carefully into her arms, draping him over her shoulders. Remembering what she'd been told the night before, she murmured, "Your name is Kos."

Kos raised his head, his forked tongue flicking, his yellow eyes with their slitted pupils looking into hers as he accepted his name.

A scuffling sound from behind her broke her concentration. She turned to look. Guy stood at the edge of the clearing staring at her, his face a mask of horror. She knelt, allowing Kos to ease onto the ground and slither away. When she rose to confront Guy she found him striding toward her.

"My God!" he exclaimed. "Are you all right?"

The power drained from Lia and she staggered, suddenly weak. When Guy wrapped his arms around her, she leaned against him gratefully.

He twisted his head to look all around. "Not a sign of that damned snake—it seemed to disappear into thin air. What were you thinking of, picking up a snake? It could have been poisonous."

Kos would never harm her. Before she could gather strength to tell him so, he muttered, "I'd better get us both out of this sun."

Brief as it had been, her assumption of power had exhausted her. She could barely walk as he led her under the magnolia canopy. He paused.

"Hold on to me while I take off my shirt for you to sit on," he said.

The dense shade provided by the ancient trees kept down the growth under them as well as offering respite from the sun's heat. Guy sat on the ground next to her and put his arm around her shoulders, making it easy for her to rest her head against his bare chest.

"I wasn't hallucinating, that *was* a snake you were holding?" As he spoke, she heard the rumble of his voice in his chest, a soothing, comforting sound.

"He was harmless," she murmured.

"I thought you were afraid of snakes," he said.

"I don't seem to be now." It was the truth. She could hardly remember whether or not she'd once feared them.

"Evidently not." He spoke dryly.

She leaned away to look up at him. "I've upset you."

"It's not every day I see a woman with a snake draped over her shoulders. Scared me to hell and gone—I was convinced the thing was going to sink its fangs into you then and there."

Lia tried to tell him about the power she'd found within her but she couldn't find a reasonable way to begin. Would he understand even if she could find the right words? She doubted it.

"It's this damned estate," he said. "Neither of us is behaving normally." He took her face between his hands, gazing tenderly at her. "I don't want to see you hurt. Ever."

His eyes were like the sun, warm and radiant, promising her—was it love? She stared bemusedly into their golden depths, wanting to believe that love awaited her in his arms, that he would never change, never again become the unwelcome other.

"You're the woman I've searched for all my life," he murmured, "and now that I've found you I won't let you go. No one will separate us." He took a deep breath, his hands leaving her face as he threw back his head and shouted defiantly, "No one!"

Above them in the magnolia, as though alarmed by his words, a large white bird took flight with a rustle of wings. Two green leaves floated down, one after the other, to rest side by side on the ground near them. The scent of jasmine drifted to them, carried on the warm breeze. Around them insects chirred.

Lia caressed the smooth magnolia leaves with her fingers. "Sulie would say these are a favorable omen."

"The trouble with Sulie is she says too much and not enough at the same time." Guy covered her hand with his. "You know I can't let you stay here alone, Lia. We have to go—"

She stopped him by putting her fingers over his lips. "Don't talk about leaving. It's too late to go. Maybe it was too late from the beginning. From the moment we set foot on de la Roche property. Or even before. Didn't you say your dreams about a woman in white began when you were a child?"

He wrapped his arms around her, pulling her to him. "How can I keep you safe from the danger here," he whispered against her lips, "when I can't be sure it won't come through me?"

With his mouth so close to hers, how could he expect her to dwell on danger? Deliberately, provocatively, she tasted his lips with the tip of her tongue, savoring the slight salty tang.

His mouth slanted over hers gently, sweetly, his kiss seeking response rather than demanding, a kiss so tender and loving there was no need for words.

Soon her rising desire would demand more but, for the moment, the kiss was everything she'd ever wanted. If only this wonderful feeling of being cherished could last forever.

When at last his lips left hers, he murmured, "Jasmine. Jasmine and you. The most romantic combination in the world." As his hand slid under her silk tank top and cupped her breast, he added, "Erotic, too."

Bemused by his caresses, she felt herself sinking into a delicious languor where time had no meaning. They had forever to explore one another, to savor every nuance of lovemaking.

Without warning a hungry, avid lust invaded her. She almost gave in to it before she realized what was happening. "No!" she cried, tearing herself away from him.

As he stared at her in consternation, she sprang to her feet and fled toward the house, knowing that if she didn't put distance between them she'd be taken over completely. By the time she rushed, breathless, through the back door, she was herself again but she couldn't be sure what would happen when he caught up to her.

On her way to the stairs she saw Sulie in the morning room. Stopping, she said, "Tell Guy I'm taking a nap and don't want to be disturbed."

After exiling herself to her room, Lia realized she was exhausted. She stretched out on the bed and closed her eyes, heartsick at how the sweetness and wonder between her and Guy had been destroyed by the other. Though she'd managed to resist being taken over completely, she knew only flight had saved her.

Why hadn't she been able to prevent the other from trying to control her? Where was the power she'd conjured up earlier? Had it been only an illusion? No, Kos had been real—Guy had seen him. But what good was the power if it couldn't keep away the other?

Fire comes next. The thought slithered into her mind as silently as Kos. *Fire defines power.*

Unsure whether to be encouraged or not, Lia clung to the thought as she slid helplessly into a deep, dreamless sleep. She woke at twilight feeling revived but surprised that she'd slept so long. Evidently power drained the user, she decided.

After washing and changing from the wraparound silk skirt and tank top she'd been wearing into a sleeveless cotton dress, she left her room, only to be brought up short by what she found on the outside of her door. Thoroughly revolted at the sight of the dead white moth affixed to the door with a pearl-headed pin, she reached up to detach it and found she couldn't bring herself to touch either pin or moth.

A white glimmer on Guy's door across the hall caught her eye and she shuddered. Was every door in the house defaced by these ghastly trophies? As she stared at his door it opened, startling her so that she bit back a cry.

"What's wrong?" Guy asked, stepping into the hall.

Wordlessly, she pointed.

"What the hell?" he muttered as he examined the pinned moths. "Sulie must have done this. God knows why."

"I don't care who did it or why," she cried. "Take them off!"

He ducked back into his room and returned with a wastebasket. Drawing out the pin, he dropped the moth from his door into the basket, then did the same with hers.

"That's not enough," she insisted. "Get rid of them altogether."

He disappeared inside once more and she heard a toilet flush. He rejoined her in the hall just as Sulie appeared.

"Those moths—" Lia began.

"You don't know nothing, you two," Sulie scolded. "Ole Miss keep trying to protect you but you don't be letting her."

"Ole Miss didn't pin those moths to our doors," Guy accused. "You did."

"Me, I never say I didn't. I do what she say. I do and you undo. Seem like you must be wanting harm to find you."

"If harm comes looking I don't think dead moths will be of much help in keeping it away," Guy said.

"Maybe nothing can help lest Miss Lia work fast to gather power," Sulie agreed. "Can't do nothing 'bout that now, time's not right. You be wanting your supper? I can stir up some dirty rice to go 'long with that leftover cold chicken."

"That sounds great," Lia said, ready to banish the moths from her mind once and for all. "I'll come down and help."

Though she wondered when the time would be right and how she was supposed to go about gathering power, she didn't bother to ask, aware that only when Sulie was ready would she tell her.

"My specialty is salad," Guy put in. "It's time I lent a hand in the kitchen, too."

"Did you call the rental car agency?" Lia asked as they went down the stairs.

Guy shrugged.

"What's that supposed to mean?" she asked.

"If you won't get in the car and come with me, I'm not going anywhere. I did find out there's taxi and limo service if you change your mind."

She couldn't deny she was tempted. At the same time she dismissed any dream of happiness with Guy somewhere away from the estate. She knew deep in her soul that could never be, not unless they first overcame and banished what threatened them here.

In the kitchen, Guy snapped on the small radio that sat on the shelf of the old-fashioned built-in corner cupboard, the only radio in the house. It belonged to

Sulie. Great-aunt Marie-Louise had no use for radios, much less TVs.

Guy found a station playing Cajun music and its lively beat seemed to lighten the room, momentarily driving away the lurking shadows.

When he finished making the salad, he took Lia by surprise, whirling her around and around in an impromptu dance.

"Where did you learn Cajun dancing?" she asked when he let her go.

"Didn't. Made it up as I went along. One of my hidden talents."

"My last man, he was Cajun," Sulie put in. "Ole Miss, she don't approve but I don't pay no mind. She be glad enough of him doing the handiwork, come to that. We got along fine mostly, Ole Miss and me, 'cept she was what they call an old maid and me, I just never got married." Sulie grinned slyly. "There be a difference."

"Like between skim milk and cream," Guy suggested.

Sulie flashed him the first approving look Lia had ever seen her give him. "De la Roche women, they be hot-blooded," she said. "Seem like the blood run real thin by the time it get to Ole Miss. May be just as well."

"Why?" Lia asked, hoping to prime Sulie's information pump.

Sulie set the platter of cold chicken on the table with a thump. "Why you think?"

"Were there unfaithful de la Roche wives back in the old days?" Lia asked.

"I 'spect so."

Lia frowned, aware she'd missed the mark. Sulie had meant something else entirely. She was trying to think of another possibility, when Sulie, after scanning the table, nodded.

"Look like everything be ready to eat," she said.

After two nights of insistent coaxing, Lia had persuaded Sulie to sit down with them—apparently she'd never eaten at the same table with Ole Miss. When they were all seated, Lia waited until everyone had food on their plates before taking up where she'd left off.

"Do you think the de la Roche woman who put the hair in the brooch was an unfaithful wife?" She asked the question of Guy rather than Sulie.

"No." He blinked, apparently taken aback by his own quick answer. "I have the feeling she wasn't," he added after a moment or two.

"Be right," Sulie said. "That one don't never marry."

Aha, Lia told herself with satisfaction. We may be getting somewhere. "Why didn't she marry?"

"She only be wanting one man. Can't have him, won't take no other."

"He didn't want her, then?" Lia persisted.

"What he be wanting he can't have no more than she can."

"There must have been a reason."

"He *be* married."

"Phillipe de la Roche was married but that didn't stop him," Guy commented. "He even fathered a second family."

Sulie shrugged. "That Phillipe, he be a de la Roche, not a—" She stopped abruptly.

"Not a Revenir?" Guy asked. "Come on, Sulie, you're not giving away any secrets by admitting a Revenir was the lady's secret lover."

She shot him a dark look. "Guess you got the right to know, seeing you got Revenir blood. The two of them, they be caught in a *rêve à deux*, couldn't never get free of it."

A shared dream but an unreal dream, according to how Sulie had translated the term. Perhaps a shared delusion? A shared obsession?

"Shared obsession," Lia said aloud, somehow sure she'd found the right phrase.

Guy stared at her. "Are you saying you think that might explain the present problem?" He spoke to Lia but Sulie answered.

"They be dead but they don't be free. Me, I don't say no more."

True to her word, Sulie didn't.

After they finished eating, Lia and Guy took over washing and drying the dishes, a familiar, homely task that became more than that because Guy was helping her. Once they were through, he led her into the library and closed the door, saying, "I don't want Sulie eavesdropping"

She leaned against the desk, watching him as he spread out the parchment with the de la Roche family tree. He moved with the grace and economy of a cat—no wasted effort. Not some tame tabby, though, not with those leopard's eyes. Did all the Revenir men have the same golden eyes?

"Here," he said, pointing to the paper in front of him. "Look, this has to be her."

Lia came close enough to peer down at the line his finger was on, aware she was reluctant and wondering why. Shouldn't she be as eager as he to pin down the ancestor who'd worn the brooch containing Revenir hair? The woman whose obsession may have transcended death?

When she saw the name Evangeline, a chill settled over her and she hugged herself, closing her eyes to blot out the name.

"Don't you agree?" Guy asked. Then, apparently noticing her distress for the first time, he put an arm around her shoulders. "What's the matter?" he asked.

"She knows we've found her name," Lia whispered, the words coming unexpectedly. "I can feel her anger."

He drew her away from the desk, pulling her down next to him on the worn leather couch. She sat stiffly, afraid to lean against him.

"I know that's why you ran from me earlier today," he said. "I could feel her try to take control."

She turned to look at him. "Did you ... change, too?"

"No. But I knew she was there."

"If I hadn't run, would you have gone on making love to me, knowing I'd changed?" Lia asked.

He hesitated before saying, "I'm not sure."

She jumped to her feet. "What kind of an answer is that?"

He smiled ruefully. "Honest. Did you want me to lie? I like to think of myself as an honorable man but when you're in my arms the truth is I can't think. On the other hand, I have no real desire to make love to long-dead Evangeline so that might have stopped me."

"Don't say her name!"

He rose and reached to take her hands but she turned from him, her voice quivering as she said, "I'm afraid to let you touch me. I'm not even sure it's safe to be in the same room with you."

"Don't ask me to go away, Lia, because I won't."

His words were tinged with anger and she knew his annoyance stemmed from the way she was acting. But she found it impossible to explain how she dreaded the thought of him making love to Evangeline instead of her. God forbid, that she'd ever make love to the other Guy, the one named Revenir.

"I don't want you to leave," she told him.

"At the same time, you don't want my company. That leaves me with the choice of taking a walk by myself, joining Sulie or going up to my room and communing with General Lafayette. Since a night walk in the jungle outside has limited appeal and trying to make sense of Sulie's cryptic conversation little more, I'll opt for the general. Good night, Lia."

At the door, he paused. "You aren't planning to go outside tonight, are you?"

She blinked in astonishment. "Heavens, no! Why would I?"

Guy hesitated, reluctant to mention the snake he'd seen her handling earlier today. He still didn't understand why she'd behaved in such an odd and frightening manner. Instead of answering her question, he said, "Why don't we both leave our bedroom doors open tonight? If you should call for help, I want to be able to hear you."

"All right. Good night, Guy."

In his hot bedroom, Guy saluted the general before stripping off his clothes and getting ready for bed. Even a sheet would be too much of a cover, he decided. He tossed a pair of pajama bottoms on the back of a chair within easy reach and climbed into bed nude with a new law thriller paperback he'd picked up at the airport when he'd arrived in New Orleans.

Thriller or not, the book failed to engross him. He tossed it aside, flicked off the light and sprawled onto his stomach, a line of poetry circling annoyingly in his mind, something about pines and hemlocks. What the hell was it? He wasn't a reader of poetry so this had to go back to college—or maybe even earlier. Finally the right words came to him:

"This is the forest primeval.
The murmuring pines and the hemlocks..."

Longfellow's *Evangeline*—no wonder it had stuck in his mind. Both he and the de la Roche Evangeline were a long way from the pines and hemlocks of a Canadian forest. By all rights, Evangeline de la Roche should be a long way from anything on earth, since she'd been dead for well over a hundred years. Dead and buried, perhaps, on these very grounds, her crypt hidden by tangled vines.

He'd never believed in ghosts or the return of spirits of the dead but there was no other explanation he could find for the insidious invasion of both Lia and himself.

Guy flung himself onto his back, aware that brooding about what had happened wasn't going to help him sleep. He forced himself to think instead about bankruptcy law in all its twists and ramifications until he finally slept.

When the woman in white invaded his dreams, for the first time he truly understood the words she whispered to him. *Je reviens. I come back.* The knowledge only increased his fear of her. Lovely and compelling, she beckoned to him and, unable, as always, to resist, he followed her as she drifted toward the sinister unknown.

When she neared the seeking tendrils of darkness, she paused and reached toward him, holding her bare white arms out, inviting him into her embrace.

Though he dreaded her touch, he couldn't resist what she offered. He drew nearer and she smiled, her pale lips tempting him at the same time he feared her kiss.

"Je reviens," she whispered again and he knew it was true. She'd returned to him as she'd promised, as she'd threatened so long ago. Come back to love him. To consume him. And he was helpless.

He stared at her hand, inches from his. He knew he was doomed when they touched and yet he yearned for her, revolted and agonized by his need. His breath caught in horror as her pale flesh began to peel away from her reaching fingers, revealing the white bones underneath.

Paralyzed with terror, he stared from her skeleton fingers to the skull that had replaced her face, mesmerized by the hellfire glowing in the sockets where her eyes should be.

"No!" he tried to shout, but the denial caught in his throat as the grinning skull swooped closer and closer....

CHAPTER EIGHT

Guy heard his name hanging like a lifeline in the air, a lifeline dangling between him and the fleshless horror that beckoned him to hell.

"Guy!" the call came again, louder and closer, blurring the reality of the hideous grinning skull and the reaching skeleton fingers. "Wake up, Guy!"

Exerting all his will, he tried to obey, fighting against the bonds that held him to the horrible vision summoning him, knowing his salvation lay in the voice that called to him.

He woke abruptly, finding himself tangled in the sheet, soaked with sweat. A figure in white stood over him and he recoiled, until the moonlight slanting in through the open window revealed Lia's concerned face.

He thrust himself up until he was sitting propped against the headboard and wiped the perspiration from his face with the sheet. Belatedly remembering he was naked, he hastily rearranged the damp sheet, draping it over his pelvis and thighs.

"I heard you thrashing and moaning," Lia said, perching on the edge of his bed. "The same nightmare?"

"Only worse," he muttered. "Much worse. At one time I thought the woman in white might be you but I know now she isn't. God, no! Never you. She's dead but she's returned, just as she's been telling me since I was a child. She's Evangeline, I know she must be, and this time..." He paused and took a deep breath, letting it out in a rush. "This time she almost—almost—" He stopped again, unsure of what would have happened if those bony fingers had touched him but knowing her touch would have been fatal.

Lia took his hand in hers. "I'm sure the nightmare must have been horrible beyond belief but bad dreams are only that—they're not real."

"Aren't they? Somehow I think this one might turn out to be." He gripped her hand hard, relieved by the feel of her warm flesh under his fingers. Lia was real, she was flesh and blood. And what she wore, though white, was a sleep-T, not the filmy nightgown from the attic, the nightgown that had been Evangeline's.

Beginning to recover somewhat, he noticed with appreciation and interest how the V-neck cotton shirt clung to her breasts and how much of her rounded thighs it revealed. He clamped down firmly on his escalating desire. At the moment just having her with him outweighed the risk of making love to her.

"Stay and talk to me for a while," he said, releasing her hand and offering her a pillow.

She glanced at the portrait on the wall. "I'm none too sure General Lafayette approves, but on the other hand, he *is* a Frenchman." She took the pillow, eased down to the end of the bed and propped herself up against the footboard.

"I wasn't asleep when I heard you moaning," she said. "I couldn't sleep. I kept thinking that if you hadn't gotten involved with me and my inheritance, you'd be safely back in Oakland instead of trapped in this living nightmare. It makes me feel guilty."

"You forget, I'd already planned a trip to New Orleans before we met," he said.

"Yes, but that was only to look for clues to your birth parents."

"You're also forgetting that because she's known all along I was the last of the Revenirs the woman in white has been invading my dreams since I was a little boy, calling to me, luring me—where? Here, of course. So you're not to blame, you're as much a victim as I am."

Lia sighed. "I once vowed I'd never be anyone's victim again. Or involve myself with any man again."

"Why? What happened to you?"

"It's the usual stupid story. I married at eighteen and it turned out to be the disaster my grandparents had predicted. They were against my marrying him from the very beginning but what teenager listens? We were both far too immature to make the marriage work but the real problem was his unreasonable jealousy.

"When he became physically abusive, I left him but he kept tracking me down and threatening me. Then he was killed in an accident and my main emotion was relief. And, of course, guilt because I felt no grief.

Except for my grandfather, I don't think I've ever really trusted a man since.''

Hearing how her voice shook as she finished, Guy longed to comfort her by taking her into his arms but he quelled the impulse and tried to find the right words instead. He failed.

"I don't know what to say," he admitted. "That was one hell of a nasty experience to suffer through— I can imagine the bitterness you felt. And I can see how it makes our situation here all the more difficult for you because, given the dark forces here, I'm certainly not a man you can trust from one minute to the next. You can't ever be quite sure if I'm your friend or the Revenir from the past.''

"I know it's not your fault," she told him.

"For all the good that does.''

"It makes a difference," she protested, edging up to put her hand on his ankle. "I know you're really my friend. *He* isn't, the other, but you are. You care what happens to me, you try to protect me.''

He wondered if she realized she was caressing him as she spoke, running her fingers up and down his lower leg. Did she have any idea what this was doing to him?

Leaning forward, he caught her wrist with his hand to stop her. "It's true I'm your friend," he said, "but I'm also a man who happens to be very attracted to you. As myself, I mean, not as some Revenir ancestor reliving an unhappy love affair.''

"I think it was more than simply an unhappy affair," she said. "Something far darker. And I know you want me, Lia, not *her*." She edged closer. "As I want you, not *him*. The wanting and the uncertainty makes me so afraid."

He couldn't resist the plea in her voice. He tossed caution aside along with the sheet and gathered her to him, easing down flat, telling himself he'd do no more than hold her close to comfort them both.

She snuggled against him, murmuring, "Just for a minute, okay? Then I'll go back to my room."

The minute passed, then another and another as they cuddled together. She fit in his arms so perfectly that even though all he could do was hold her, he still never wanted to let her go.

"Mmm," she said softly. "I could fall asleep like this, except for one thing."

"What's the one thing?"

"Since you're totally naked it's not all that difficult to tell sleep isn't what *you* have in mind." She shifted slightly, pressing her thigh against his arousal.

Involuntarily he pulled her closer, thrusting his leg between her thighs. "I hate to disillusion you but that's not my mind you're fooling around with down there."

"No? I'm sure I read somewhere that men think with a different part of their anatomy than women do."

His laugh was low and husky. "As a naked man, I'm in no condition to argue." His hand eased under the edge of her short sleep-T and caressed the curve of her bare hip. "You aren't exactly overdressed yourself. Not that I'm complaining."

Without another word, he covered her lips with his, savoring the sweetness of her mouth, gradually deepening the kiss, relishing her soft sounds of pleasure and need, assured that Lia wanted him as much as he wanted her.

He broke the kiss to push her shirt up until he could pull it over her head and off. The brush of her breasts against his chest sent a wild surge of need through him. He cupped both her breasts in his hands, rubbing his thumbs across her swollen nipples until she pressed her hips against him, moaning.

"So beautiful," he whispered. "Beautiful Lia."

He couldn't tell whether the jasmine he smelled came from her skin or from the open window but its perfume blended with her own scent to intoxicate him as he trailed his lips along her throat and down to her breast.

Her hands tangled in his hair as she arched to him, showing him she felt the same exciting need that pounded through him. When he rose over her, her body, moist and pliant under his hands, opened to welcome him.

"Ah, Lia, Lia," he groaned as he eased into her warmth, gently at first, then harder and faster as she enclosed him within her.

They moved together, joined in the sweetly urgent rhythm of their combined desire and need, lost to everything but one another. And when at last they returned, sated, to reality, he still held her, reluctant to let her go.

"You and me," she murmured drowsily. "You and me."

He knew exactly what she meant. They'd been themselves, Lia Courtois and Guy Russell, and he'd never made such perfect love with anyone. Relaxed, happier than he could ever remember being, he started to doze.

Laughter woke him. A woman's laughter, low, throaty and triumphant. In his arms, Lia was laughing. Why didn't it sound like Lia? Apprehension tensed him, but, before he could move, an insidious wave of lust rose in him. In the sickening instant before he became oblivious to all else but the naked woman in his arms, he realized what was happening. But it was too late.

He stared down at her, the moon's rays showing him her lustrous black hair spilling over the pillow and the moon's light silvering her soft white skin. She looked up at him, her smile mocking him, taunting him.

"Witch," he muttered, burning with the need to master her, to turn her into a mere woman, one he could take or leave alone.

Pulling her roughly to him, he kissed her savagely, a kiss as full of hate as it was lust. Her response was wild and passionate with her teeth cutting into his lips while her tongue lapped the blood. He countered by pulling away and taking her breast into his mouth, his teeth nibbling at her nipple until she screamed with mixed pleasure and pain.

He caught her to him again, his kiss fierce and probing, his hands molding her body to his. His fingers found her center, as hot and throbbing with need as he was. Shoving her legs apart he plunged into her. She dug her fingernails into his back and wrapped herself around him like a snake, writhing and twisting as his thrusting grew more and more violent.

When she reached the peak she shrieked like one of the catamints in the swamp beyond the bayou and her cry, as it always did, triggered him into his own molten release.

As soon as he could, he rolled away from her, despising himself for succumbing to her lure, loathing her power over him. How many times had he vowed not to come near her again? He'd never yet been able to keep that vow. Damn her for a witch!

He slid from the bed and reached for his breeches. . . .

Guy stood beside the bed staring in confusion at the pajama bottoms he held in his hand. And then the awful truth hit him. The other had taken control of him. He drew in his breath and swung around to look at Lia. How could she ever forgive him? And yet—had she been Lia? He knew she couldn't have been.

She lay huddled in the tangled sheets, her back to him. He tried to say her name but had to clear his throat before any sound emerged. "Lia?"

"It makes me ashamed." Her words were so muffled he could hardly hear her.

"It wasn't your fault." He stepped closer and tentatively touched her shoulder.

She jerked away and sat up, clutching the damp sheet to her. "I know that. It was her, not me. Evangeline. Isn't it bad enough she takes me over? Why must she force me to remember what she makes me do?"

"I wasn't myself, either," he muttered, glancing away from her, trying not to recall what they'd been forced to do. But his lips stung from being bitten and so did the fingernail scratches on his back. He winced when he thought of the bruises Lia must have.

He started to sit on the edge of the bed, then decided Lia might feel more secure if he wasn't naked so he slid into his pajama bottoms.

"I won't touch you," he assured her as he eased onto the bed.

"I think I'd feel safer in my own room," she said. "Please don't look."

Understanding that she wanted to put on her sleep-T, he turned away from her. He tried to find words to tell her that the violent lust they'd been forced to engage in couldn't alter the sweetness of their own by-choice lovemaking but nothing he came up with sounded right.

"I'm as upset as you are," he said finally. "Especially since I've just realized something. As you know,

I used protection." Guy turned to glance at her. "*He* didn't. Are you on—?"

Lia gave him an appalled look, shook her head and burst into tears. Much as he longed to hold her, he knew she was afraid to have him touch her. With good reason. They didn't dare risk the chance that even a casual touch could trigger a takeover. Frustrated rage simmered inside him.

"We leave this damn place at dawn," he announced.

"We'll never get away from them," Lia sobbed. "They'll follow us wherever we go."

"You can't be sure of that."

She sniffed and wiped her tear-streaked face with the sheet. "Didn't she already find you in Oakland when you were just a child? She has power. She'll come after us. And she'll bring him with her. We have to stay and fight them here."

"How?"

"You fight power with power. Sulie's right—I have to learn how to use mine in a hurry. I think Kos will be able to help me."

About to ask who the hell Kos was, he remembered the snake. Chances were she would never be able to find the same snake again and, even if she did, what did she think a snake could do? "Have you gone crazy?" he demanded.

She ignored his words. "And fire. Sulie will have to tell me how to use the fire. I'm sure she knows—I'll make her tell me."

"Lia," he said, concerned, "I don't think—"

She fixed her gaze on him, her dark eyes gleaming in the moonlight. "You'll have to stay here with me even though it puts you in danger. I don't yet understand why, but I know my power won't be effective if you leave. This isn't merely between me and Evangeline. You and the other Guy are also a part—the four of us are caught in a trap."

Deciding if he humored her perhaps in time she'd recognize this talk of power and snakes and fire was skewed thinking, he said, "My Revenir ancestor hates her. Maybe I ought to try to get him on my side. Our side."

He could see that Lia was considering what he'd said, to his consternation obviously taking him seriously. "That's not a bad idea," she told him. "If you can figure out a way."

He stared at her, at a loss. How the hell could she expect him to make contact with a spirit, much less convince it—no, him—to help them?

"Good night," she said. "I'm going to my room. I really believe we're better off staying apart."

He couldn't deny the logic of that. He watched her leave, belatedly realizing his door had been open all this time. Considering the noise they'd made after being claimed by the others it's a wonder Sulie hadn't come to investigate.

He still was inclined to leave but not without Lia. Wasn't it possible, though, that she was right about Evangeline's ability to follow? Perhaps fleeing from this haunted place wasn't the solution. But neither was Kos, the snake. Or fire.

He stripped the damp sheets from the bed and stretched out on the mattress pad, hands behind his head, staring at Lafayette's portrait. History had been his minor at Stanford and he'd always admired this aristocratic Frenchman who'd risked his life to help the American colonists fight for their freedom from Britain.

"So, what did you do during the Revolution when the battle turned against you, general?" he asked.

The last thing Guy was aware of before he slipped over the edge into sleep was the Marquis de Lafayette's inscrutable gaze fixed on him....

Tents rose to the right and left of him but no camp-fires burned, lest the enemy spot their night position. A fire would have been welcome for, though spring in Virginia was warm, the fall of night brought a chill to the air. He'd never expected to become a soldier, strange how fate altered a man's life.

The tent flap in front of him pushed open and he sprang to attention. "Sir," he said, saluting the tall and slim uniformed general who emerged from the tent. "Any orders, sir?"

"At ease." Lafayette spoke English with a marked accent. "Has any runner returned with additional information about General Clinton's deployment of troops?"

"No, sir. No more than we already know—that the British forces greatly outnumber ours."

Lafayette nodded gloomily and began to limp up and down in front of the tent, favoring the leg that had been wounded at Brandywine. He watched the general, finally gathering courage to ask the question that had long troubled him.

"What will you do, sir?"

Lafayette stopped and eyed him for a long moment before he made any answer. "Were I to fight a battle I should be cut to pieces. Not to fight at all is unthinkable. I am therefore determined to skirmish."

As he thought over the general's words, Lafayette reentered the tent, leaving him alone. Skirmish? he thought, dispiritedly. Not face up to battle? But I need to win, not merely harass the enemy.

Then don't ask advice of generals. The voice came from nowhere, from everywhere, making him glance wildly around. He saw no one and finally accepted that he heard the words only in his mind.

This is a family affair, is it not? the voice inquired.

Family? Americans fighting to be free of Britain?

The war is a dream. Your fight is not. If you need help, ask one who might have cause to listen.

The tents blurred and faded, disappearing. He stood alone in darkness. "I need help," he admitted.

When the time comes, heed my words so we may fight together, you and I. We fight together or the battle is lost—forever.

Guy woke in confusion, the words he'd heard spinning in his head. Had someone reached out to him from the past or was it no more than a dream within a dream?

Had he been offered hope or was hope only another illusion?

CHAPTER NINE

When Lia came down to breakfast, she found Guy already at the kitchen table sipping coffee and talking to Sulie. "Me, I tell you ain't nobody seen that grave for years and years," Sulie was saying when she walked in.

As Lia sat down, Guy shot her a quick smile before focusing on Sulie once more. "Since the shrubbery's been allowed to run wild, I don't doubt that but I didn't ask you if anyone had seen the grave lately, I asked you where it was. Surely the location hasn't changed."

"Be in the same place. Between the *garçonnière* and the bayou."

"Between the bayou and what?" Guy asked.

"Garçonnière," Sulie repeated. "In old times, men who don't be married sleep there, don't sleep in the house."

"Like bachelor quarters," Lia suggested, spreading peach jam on the French toast Sulie set before her.

"I thought I'd look for Evangeline's crypt," Guy told Lia. "If it *is* hers." He glanced at Sulie.

Sulie rubbed her arms as though the morning was chilly instead of overwarm, then clutched at the high neck of her dress. "Don't like hearing her name said right out like that," she said. "Won't do no good to go poking 'round that grave, neither."

"Is it hers?" Lia asked bluntly.

Sulie's nod was reluctant. "Be a storm coming. I feel it."

Lia assumed the abrupt mention of weather was Sulie's way of trying to end the discussion about Evangeline. To her surprise, after a few moments, Sulie said, "She be calling that storm to come here 'cause her power get stronger when it storm."

"The news on the radio this morning didn't mention bad weather," Guy said.

"It be coming," Sulie repeated. "You wait, you be seeing a storm."

"What I'd like to see is the *garçonnière*," Lia said, deciding the subject really did need to be changed. "I didn't know there was one on the grounds."

"It be by the oak grove in back—that way." Sulie pointed to what would be the left if they went out the kitchen door. "The trees, they grow 'round, shut it in like a cage."

"Did Aunt Marie-Louise ever use it?"

"Never. Nobody go in that bad place for years."

"Bad place?" Guy echoed.

"Don't feel right inside, Ole Miss tell me."

Lia knew better than to suggest Marie-Louise might have meant the *garçonnière* had fallen into such disrepair that it might prove dangerous to enter. Nothing on this estate ever seemed to have a simple explanation.

"Once we reach the old bachelor quarters," Guy said, "we can locate the bayou and that ought to give us a pretty good idea of where to find the crypt. By all means, let's visit the *garçonnière*."

Us, he kept saying, meaning the two of them. As she finished her coffee, Lia told herself it was probably safe enough to be alone with Guy during the day, providing they were careful to avoid touching—and she meant to be very, very careful. She'd worn a loose shirt over an old pair of jeans, covering last night's bruises, but out of sight wasn't out of mind. She remembered all too well how she'd come by those bruises.

"If we're going, we'd best get started before it's too hot," she said.

Once outside, the steamy summer heat rose around them, making Lia wonder how it could possibly get any hotter. Summer obviously wasn't the best time to be in Louisiana.

When they reached the shelter of overhanging branches she expected the shade would offer some relief but, though they were protected from the sun, the thick growth shut away any stray breeze and it remained stifling.

"I really don't understand why Aunt Marie-Louise didn't hire gardeners," Lia said, using a tissue to wipe her forehead as she followed Guy deeper into the greenery.

"Apparently the money's there," Guy said, "because Bob LaBranche agreed quickly enough to having the estate hire one." He was silent for a time before saying, without turning to look at her, "Are you all right?"

She knew what he meant. "Yes. Just don't touch me."

"Don't worry, I won't."

Perversely, because she was sure he meant what he said, she found herself admiring the powerful flex of his arm muscles as he hacked at the growth with a meat cleaver from the kitchen. Since he was wearing the sleeves of his green T-shirt rolled up, she had an excellent view. Her gaze traveled approvingly down his snug-fitting jeans until what she was thinking brought her up short—fantasies were dangerous.

How could she forget the violation of being taken over last night and forced to enact another woman's fantasy? Before that, though, when they'd been themselves, she and Guy... No, she wouldn't think about that, either. It might not be safe.

"We're nearing the oaks," he said.

She saw the arched branches of the trees, branches festooned with Spanish moss, above the tangle of overgrowth impeding their passage. Soon, through the greenery ahead, she caught a glimpse of weathered white boards—the *garçonnière*.

"In the old days did they make the bachelors sleep away from the house because they didn't trust them inside?" she wondered aloud.

"I thought maybe the idea was to offer the gentlemen some privacy."

"Privacy meaning what my grandmother would call up to no good?"

"Wine and song, anyway."

"You left out what goes between. I doubt if they did."

He looked back to flash her a grin. "Maybe that's why Ole Miss called it a bad place."

When they finally came on the old building, octagonal like the gazebo, she sighed with disappointment. Though the deep shade under the oaks discouraged the growth of lesser plants, over the years the trees themselves had damaged the *garçonnière,* smashing in the sides of the upper story and causing the roof to settle down over what must be the first floor.

Guy found the door and turned its brass knob. The door wasn't locked but he had difficulty pushing it open. "Out of alignment," he muttered, peering cautiously inside.

"Is it safe to go in?" she asked.

"The floor's intact. Doesn't seem to be much water damage—the roof must be keeping out most of the rain. Strange how it settled so evenly and all of a piece after the second floor went."

He moved farther inside, out of the doorway, and she slipped through, eager to see what remained of the place. Light shone dim and greenish through the cracked and dirty windows. The entry and the two rooms to either side were empty, their doors wide open.

The door to the middle room was closed, with a brass key in its lock. She tried the knob but the door wouldn't open. She touched the key with hesitant fingers.

"Maybe you should leave it as is," Guy suggested. "Then you can use your imagination to furnish the unseen room instead of being disappointed when you find it's as empty as the others."

How perceptive he was—she hadn't thought he'd noticed how let down she'd felt when she saw the other two rooms.

But she was too curious to take his suggestion. Tightening her grip on the key, she turned it in the lock and opened the door.

The smell of musk mingled with the musty odor already present in the *garçonnière*. Lia peered into the shadowy room, then took a step inside. The only light in the cypress-paneled octagonal room filtered through narrow, colored glass windows set horizontally at the junction of walls and ceiling.

Though the room was furnished, rot and decay had all but destroyed the once elegant carpet and the fabrics covering the chairs. A large chaise longue occupied the center of the room, its red velvet upholstery faded and marred by a large rusty stain that also marked the carpet beneath the chaise. Gazing at it, unable to look away, she felt an inexplicable chill of horror.

"Whoever painted this was damn good," Guy commented. His voice broke the spell. With relief, she turned to see him examining one of the eight oil paintings that hung, one to each octagonal panel, on the walls.

Joining him, she stared at the gold-framed painting of a man bending over a woman in a negligee who reclined on a chaise very much like the one in the room. Both were appealingly sensual as well as obviously attracted to one another.

"I think the man has auburn hair, though it's difficult to tell in this light," Guy said. He ran his finger gently over the man's head, leaving a lighter streak where he'd wiped away accumulated dirt. Lia nodded. Auburn hair.

The woman's long, wavy black hair cascaded over her scantily draped shoulders and breasts. "I wonder if she's supposed to be Evangeline and he's her Revenir lover," she said.

Guy was already studying the next painting. "Could be," he said, "though idealized by the artist. The same couple's in this one."

The man was now sitting on the edge of the chaise gazing into the woman's eyes. She was lifting a hand toward his face. The artist had caught the sexual tension between the two, making it all but palpable.

In the third picture they were locked in a heated, fervent kiss. Lia caught her breath as she looked at the fourth. The woman's negligee was open and her parted lips and passion-dazed eyes showed how much she enjoyed the man's hand caressing her bared breast.

"The seduction is progressing," Guy murmured, pausing to look at her. "Maybe we ought to forego the last four—I think we can guess what they'll show."

She suspected he was right. Viewing the complete seduction might be as unwise as flinging herself into Guy's arms would be. Yet driven by the same perversity she'd felt earlier, she drifted toward the next painting, saying, "One more."

The man's shirt was off, crumpled on the carpet beside the chaise, and the woman was entirely nude, her negligee thrown aside. His mouth was at her breast, one hand spread at the juncture of her thighs. Lia's tongue moistened her lips, imagining for an indescribable moment that she was the woman in the picture, she was the one experiencing the exquisite torture of his lips and tongue, she was the one feeling the rush of heat where his hand caressed her.

She swallowed, taking a step back, then another before colliding with Guy who'd come up behind her. He caught her around the waist to steady her and, without warning the warmth inside her spread throughout her body. She started to lean into him but something within told her the time wasn't ripe. Not yet, but soon.

She freed herself and caught his hand, pulling him with her.

In the next painting the lacings of the man's breeches were undone and the woman's long, pale fingers caressed him. His head was thrown back as he gasped in pleasure. Glancing at Guy, she saw him shift his shoulders as though trying to throw off the effect of the picture.

She smiled, satisfied that the paintings exerted their usual influence over him. There were still two more. By the time they reached the last, he'd be more than ready. Tugging at his hand, she drew him with her to the seventh painting where both man and woman were naked.

The man knelt on the chaise between the woman's spread legs, poised to commit them both to the ultimate pleasure. Though he was a magnificent specimen, he was no more so than the man beside her, the man who would soon be pleasuring her and himself. Soon, soon, for there was but one last painting. He'd never been able to resist the final scene; he wouldn't be able to now. Tingling with anticipation, she led the way to the eighth picture and raised her gaze to it.

She gasped, her hand flying to her mouth. The canvas gaped apart in its ornate frame, slashed from corner to corner in a gigantic X. The shock brought her back to herself, banishing the desire that had consumed her, making her realize that somehow she'd allowed Evangeline to assume control. Panic gripped her and she reeled dizzily. Had he also been taken over? Which Guy stood beside her?

"Lia?" His voice seemed to come from a distance as her surroundings began to fade away. The last thing she felt was his hand grip her arm.

She roused to find herself lying under the oaks with Guy kneeling beside her. "You passed out in there." He nodded toward the *garçonnière*. "No wonder—it was stifling inside plus that stink of musk."

Lia blinked at him, remembering. "The smell of sin," she muttered. A chill slithered along her spine. That didn't sound like something she'd say—had she been influenced by Evangeline?

He raised his eyebrows. "I wasn't aware sin had any particular smell."

She eased onto one elbow and he helped her to sit up, supporting her against him. "Those paintings," she began, then paused, unsure. "There *were* pictures?"

"Very erotic ones. Seven intact, one mutilated," he confirmed.

Apparently he hadn't been taken over as she had been. And he didn't seem to realize Evangeline had come to her inside the *garçonnière*. She opened her mouth to tell him and found herself too ashamed to admit what had happened to her.

"They must have met and made love in that room, your ancestor and mine," Guy said.

She shuddered inwardly, aware of how close they'd come to doing the same. If the eighth painting hadn't been destroyed, she would have been forced to seduce Guy right there in that decaying, rotting room. The very idea nauseated her.

"I have a feeling," Guy said, "that he, my ancestor, was guilty of slashing the last painting."

She nodded, thinking it quite possible Evangeline finally might have goaded him too far. *Witch,* he'd called her, during that frightening episode in the attic, using the word's more sinister meaning.

"I told you their affair was dark and driven," she said.

"Hate mixed with desire—a dangerous combination, one that doesn't let them rest in peace."

"Or give us much rest, either," she said bitterly.

He hugged her to him for an instant, then let her go. "If you think you're up to walking, we'd better get you back to the house."

"You're giving up your search for the grave?" she asked, as he helped her to her feet.

"For now."

Later, sitting with him in the morning room sipping Sulie's just-tart-enough limeade, Lia put down her glass and leaned back in her chair. "You came to New Orleans to search for your birth parents and what did you find? A Revenir ancestor who torments you. You'd have been better off not knowing."

"Exactly what my Uncle Tim warned me might happen." Guy shook his head. "I had to make the search and, though I realize I'll never know who my mother was, I did turn up a likely father, quite probably the Tanguay Revenir who was the last of the line.

"But more important, my discovery of a probable birth father has made me realize how lucky I was to be chosen by my adoptive parents. I've forgiven them for not telling me I wasn't their natural child because I've come to understand they acted as they did because they loved me and thought it best I shouldn't know."

"Do you think your birth parents were married to each other?"

He shook his head. "I doubt it. I think my mother, for some reason I'll never learn, ran away from my father. Far away, since she wound up in Oakland."

"If she did, I'm not sure I blame her. Revenirs are strange men."

He smiled wryly. "You must admit the de la Roche women are a bit weird, too."

Sulie marched into the room. "That radio weatherman, he say there be a tropical disturbance in the Gulf. Won't know nothing more, he say, for another day but I know. Gonna turn into a bad storm, maybe a hurricane, and gonna head straight for New Orleans. I *told* you she be calling up a storm." Sulie fixed her gaze on Lia. "We got maybe two days before the storm. Moon be near enough to full tomorrow night. You be ready."

Lia nodded. "I'll be ready. And so will Kos."

Sulie smiled. "Me, I knew you'd find him."

Lia smiled in return. "Kos found me."

"Gonna be all right, you hear?" Without waiting for an answer, Sulie left the room.

"What was that all about?" Guy asked.

"I've told you before—calling up power and learning how to use it. Kos will teach me about snakes and Sulie will teach me about fire. The rest is up to me."

"Are you serious?" Disbelief tinged his voice.

"I have to match, then surpass Evangeline's power."

"While I sit around watching?"

Lia shook her head. "Don't mock me. You know perfectly well the danger we're in. You said you were going to ask your ancestor for help. Have you tried?"

"I didn't really mean—" Guy paused, looking reflective. "I guess maybe I did make contact," he said at last.

The phone rang and Lia sprang up to answer it. When she returned she said, "That was Fred Speer, the gardener Mr. LaBranche contacted. He'll be out to take a look at the grounds in the morning. Sulie reminded me earlier that the cleaning crew is also due tomorrow for their once-a-month, top-to-bottom clean sweep. She says two men and two women come from this agency Aunt Marie-Louise signed up with several years ago. Using their own equipment, they go over the whole house, mopping, dusting, vacuuming and whatever else needs to be done."

"Sounds like a good day to stay out from underfoot. We could take a taxi into the city—"

Lia shook her head, stopping him. "You still don't understand, do you? We can't leave the estate until we've won."

"A trip into town isn't the same as going away for good," he pointed out.

"We can't go."

"You mean you won't."

She folded her arms. "There's no point in arguing."

He rose to face her. "Why are you so stubborn?"

"Why don't you try to understand?"

"I swear I'm tempted to sling you over my shoulder and carry you off."

She bristled. "Just you try it!"

Before she realized what he meant to do, he scooped her off her feet and she found herself facedown over his shoulder, exactly as he'd threatened. His grip on her legs prevented her from kicking, but she pounded on his back with her fists.

"Let me down!" she cried.

He ignored her. Carrying her from the morning room, he trotted up the stairs and into her bedroom. He dumped her unceremoniously onto her bed, then hooked his thumbs in the pockets of his jeans and grinned down at her. "Never challenge me," he advised.

"You damn Revenir," she snapped at him as she scrambled to sit up.

His grin faded and his cat's eyes took on a feral glow. He leaned toward her and she tried to scoot away but his hands clamped down onto her shoulders, holding her in place. "Don't call me that! Are you trying to force me into being him? Do you like having your clothes ripped off? Do you enjoy being taken by force?"

"No," she whispered, afraid of what she'd awakened in him.

"In that decaying hole where they rendezvoused, you dragged me from one of those damn pictures to the next," he growled. "You must have known the effect it would have on me. What if he'd surfaced? Did you want to be taken on that filthy floor?"

"No, but *she* did," Lia said, blurting out the truth.

His eyes flickered, the glitter waning. His grip on her shoulders eased. "She was there?" he asked.

Lia nodded, watching him warily. "Until we came to the slashed painting—then she left me."

"Oh, God." He sat on the bed and drew her into his arms.

She tensed, but when he did nothing but hold her, she relaxed against him, knowing he was himself. She desperately needed what comfort she dared to grasp.

"I'll never hurt you," he said hoarsely. "Not as long as I'm myself."

Since she couldn't count on that from one minute to the next, Lia pulled free and looked at him sadly. "I didn't even realize she'd taken me over in that foul room, not until she vanished. She was going to make me seduce you."

A smile warmed his eyes. "You don't know how much I'd enjoy being seduced by you. By Lia."

Her despair lifted as she realized what fun seducing him could be. But only if the seduction was her choice, not the choice of the other. "I'll file that away for future reference," she told him. "In the same pigeon-hole with your last name—Russell. I won't call you by the other name again."

"My last name was given to me by a man who loved me," he said. "I'll never change it." He rose. "Sitting on your bed with you is asking for trouble and we've had enough of that without inviting more." At the door he paused and looked back at her. "Do you actually *feel* this whatever-it-is power Sulie keeps telling you about?"

"Not all the time. But I've proved to myself that I do have power. If I learn how to use this power against Evangeline—" She paused. "No, not if. When. I *will* learn. There's no choice. Try to believe in me."

He shook his head. "I don't mean to be negative but toying with snakes and fire under a full moon is not my usual agenda."

Lia frowned. "Toying? Do you think I'm playing some childish game? I'm not, any more than the forces that control us are playing games."

"Will it help to say I'm convinced that you believe in what you're doing? And I hope your belief is justified by the results."

She smiled reluctantly. "The way you say things sometimes tends to persuade me that lawyers are born, not made." She gestured toward the white-and-gold dressing table near the door. "Toss me my brush before you go out, will you please?"

Guy reached for the brush and froze, staring at the top of the dressing table. Drawing back his hand, he scowled at her. "What in hell," he demanded, "are you doing with Evangeline's brooch in your room?"

CHAPTER TEN

Shortly before midnight, Guy entered his room reluctantly. Though he was tired because he hadn't slept well since God knows when, he was wary of going to bed. If he did sleep, he might dream. If he dreamed it might be of the woman in white. If he dreamed of her— He clamped off that thought.

The day had been one frustration after another. First there'd been the near-disaster in the *garçonnière*. Then came the shock of discovering that damn brooch in Lia's room. Her dismay had quickly convinced him she had no idea how Evangeline's brooch got from its box inside the chest in the library to her dressing table.

When asked, Sulie denied knowing anything about it. "Me, I don't be messing with what belong to the Dread One. Never!"

He and Lia finally concluded that Evangeline had been responsible, though Lia had no memory of being taken over and retrieving the brooch from the secret compartment in the library. Neither of them could understand why she would want Lia to find the brooch and bring it to her room. But if Evangeline wasn't responsible, who—or what—was?

The brooch was now back in its proper place. He wished he could say the same for himself. He no longer felt that he *had* a proper place, a place where he belonged. Oakland, his uncles, his law practice seemed like some far-off dream.

"You're walking around in a daze, Russell," he chided himself. "Make a plan, then follow it."

He sat on the bed gazing absently at the general and decided his first priority was to get Lia to safety. Which meant away from here, away from the estate, away from New Orleans and Louisiana.

Maybe they'd be followed by the dark forces, as she believed would happen—but she could be wrong. They'd never know unless he got them both out of here.

Next was how to do it. Kidnap her while she slept? No chance, she'd rouse and he'd have a struggle on his hands. He'd tried slinging her over his shoulder once and that certainly wouldn't work. Persuasion? He shook his head. He'd tried to persuade her more than once only to fetch up hard against the stone wall of her conviction they couldn't leave. Trickery? A possibility, if he could come up with something clever.

He needed an ally. Sulie was out. Rebecca? No, she wouldn't be effective. Worse, she might sabotage any plan because she secretly wanted Lia to remain where she was. That left Maurice. Lia liked him, a plus. He wasn't sure what Maurice could do or say that might be convincing to Lia but, if Maurice drove to the estate, there'd at least be a car available. Getting Maurice here would mean a secret phone call, though. With his door and Lia's door open, he couldn't go down to the entry without her hearing him.

He rose, went into the hall and called through Lia's open door that he was going down for some ice water—did she want some?

She didn't.

Some minutes later, he carried a glass of ice water up the stairs and into his room, satisfied that Maurice would arrive tomorrow morning. He was almost certain Lia hadn't heard him make the call.

Feeling encouraged about his chances of bringing Lia to safety, he drank the water, pulled off his pajama bottoms, turned out his light and sprawled nude onto the bed. For a while he couldn't relax but eventually fatigue caught up to him and he dropped into the dark well of sleep.

He heard her voice first, heard her whispered, *"Je reviens,"* but saw no one. Since he stood on a featureless gray plain there was no place to hide, nowhere to run. He had no choice but to wait. Wisps of mist drifted toward him, coalescing as they neared, gradually assuming a woman's form, a woman with flowing dark hair who was dressed in a white gown no more substantial than the mist.

She smiled and beckoned to him. Resistance was impossible. He was destined to follow where she led, so follow he must, follow her toward the darkness waiting at the edge of the plain.

He'd gone this way so often, lured by the woman in white. Would this be the time he'd be drawn into the darkness by her, never to return? Beneath his ever-present fear of what would happen, he marked a change. The journey took much longer than usual, the darkness seemed farther away. She drifted slowly onward and he followed after, step by reluctant step.

He'd never asked why she returned to him night after night. He now understood the answer was hidden deep within him, in his very blood, hidden from him until she chose to reveal why she led him into darkness. If she chose to tell him.

On and on she drifted, closer and closer to the evil that waited to consume him. Helpless, he followed. . . .

Lia woke with a start, certain she'd heard an unusual noise. From Guy's room? She sat and swung her legs over the edge of the bed, listening, hearing only the squeaks and croaks of insects and frogs through her open window.

She stood, slid her feet into slippers, and padded to her open door. No sound came from Guy's room. It came to her that what had roused her was a door closing so she crossed the hall to see if he'd shut his door. Finding it open, she peered into the room. A silver swathe of moonlight lay across his bed. His empty bed.

"Guy?" she called, hurrying into the room. "Are you here?" There was no answer.

After making sure he wasn't in the room or the bathroom, she ran along the hall and down the stairs, calling his name, fear rising higher in her with each step she took. The front door was locked. As she reached the kitchen, she heard footsteps on the back stairs and turned to see if it was Guy. The door at the bottom of the stairs swung open and Sulie, wearing a voluminous blue nightgown, walked into the kitchen, carrying an object wrapped in tissue paper.

"I can't find Guy!" Lia cried as she hurried to check the back door. Unlocked, it swung open. She bit her lip. "I'm worried. He has these awful nightmares and I'm afraid he may be out there in the night, walking in his sleep."

Sulie nodded. "The Dread One, she called him. He be following her to the bayou."

"No! She can't have him!"

"Wait!" Sulie's voice stopped Lia on the threshold. "Take this." The old woman held out the wrapped package she carried, pulling away the paper as she offered it to Lia.

Lia stared at crumbling flowers in an ancient wreath. "What is it?"

"It be off her grave. Use it when you need to. And don't you never look her in the eye, you hear?"

Wreath in hand, Lia rushed from the house. Though no voice spoke to her, somehow she knew Kos was guiding her as she plunged recklessly along the path she'd followed when she met him. Unseen growth brushed against her, slapping into her face and tangling around her ankles.

The night had grown ominously silent—no night insects chirred, no frogs sang. Instead of sweet jasmine, the dank breeze carried the odor of decay.

"Guy!" she called, over and over. "Guy!"

At first he thought the white wraith spoke his name. She'd only whispered to him before, what need did she have to call him when he was already following her? Then he realized the voice calling his name was someone else's, coming from somewhere other than the gray plain leading to hell's darkness.

As soon as that became clear to him, he woke—and found himself in a continuing nightmare. It was night and the moon was setting. He was not in his bed in his room, he wasn't even in the house but outside, struggling through the overgrowth toward what he knew was the bayou. He tried to stop and turn back but he could not.

Then he saw her floating ahead of him, the woman in white, his dream wraith, the Dread One, no longer confined to his dream but a terrible reality. She stretched out a pale hand and beckoned to him. He had no more choice awake than in the dream. He followed her.

He heard Lia calling, "Guy, stop! Come back!" It made no difference. He could obey only the Dread One. Lia couldn't help him. No one could.

Anger mixed with Lia's horror as she stared at the misty whiteness leading Guy toward the bayou. That ghastly thing had no right to him! Determined to stop him from following the wraith, she asked herself how it was possible. He didn't seem to hear her pleas—what could she do?

Increasing her pace she caught up to him, grasped his arm and dug in her heels, doing her best to make him halt. Without so much as glancing her way, he shook her off and continued to trail after the Dread One, moving slowly but inexorably toward the bayou's dark waters.

Calling to him had no effect. Force wouldn't work because he was stronger than she was. What now? Attack the source?

Lia fixed her gaze on the eerie woman in white and shuddered. How could she bring herself to confront what she thought of as an evil spirit? But to save Guy, she must do just that.

Gathering her courage, she sprang ahead of him, slowing as she neared the ghostly figure. Due to her fear, what she'd intended as a defiant shout of "No!" emerged as a croaking whisper.

Terror thrummed through her as she watched the wraith stop and turn toward her. Blazing eyes focused on her, paralyzing her will. Belatedly recalling Sulie's warning, with great effort, she closed her eyes and flung the crumbling wreath blindly at the Dread One.

Lia wasn't sure what she'd expected to happen. To hear a thunderclap and smell brimstone? To be annihilated? When nothing at all occurred, she finally dared to open her eyes. There was no sign of the woman in white. Was it possible Sulie's wreath had routed the Dread One?

Behind her Guy said, "Lia?" in a dazed voice.

She turned to him and grasped his arm, crying, "Run for the house!"

But it wasn't possible to run through the tangled growth. As fast as they could, they made their way though the greenery while the frogs once more took up their nightly chorus. Lia, reassured by the familiar sound, began to believe they might be safe, after all.

"Damn it, I'm naked," Guy said, sounding acutely uncomfortable.

"That's your own fault," she told him a bit crossly. "In strange houses you ought to wear at least your pajama bottoms to bed."

"I'll admit yours is the strangest house I've ever been in." He glanced over his shoulder.

"She's not following," Lia said. "She's gone."

"What was it you chucked at her?"

"Sulie said it was a wreath from the grave. Her grave. It looked old enough to be."

"Whatever it was, when it hit her she vanished like smoke in the wind."

Lia wished the Dread One would stay vanished but she knew her wish was futile. They might be safe for the moment but it wouldn't last.

When they reached the back door, Sulie was waiting. Without a word, she handed Guy his pajama bottoms. Turning his back, he put them on.

Sulie nodded toward the coffeemaker, said, "Tomorrow night," to Lia and left them.

The smell of fresh coffee chased the remaining dregs of the nightmare from Guy's head. "I don't want to go back to bed," he said as he filled two mugs and handed one to her. "How about you?"

"Not yet. The library?"

He nodded.

When they reached the library, they sat side by side on the old leather couch. Lia curled her legs up under her while Guy stretched his out and rested his feet on a stool, absently regarding the scratches and cuts.

She watched him take several swallows of coffee before saying, "Sulie knew the Dread One had lured you outside. She met me at the door with that wreath."

He glanced at her. "I won't ask how Sulie knew because I'm sure that's one of the many secrets she reveals to no one. How did *you* know?"

"I woke up when you closed the back door. I wasn't as certain as Sulie was about why you'd gone out."

He finished the coffee and set the mug on the floor. "My nightmare has shifted to reality. You saw her, didn't you?"

"White, as insubstantial as mist—until she looks at you." Lia hugged herself, unable to describe the terror she'd felt when she'd gazed at the flaming eyes of the Dread One.

"If you hadn't found me, if you hadn't stopped her—"

"Don't," Lia begged. "No more, not tonight."

He remained silent for a time. "Now what?" he asked at last. "Do you still insist on staying here?"

She glared at him. "You can't actually believe I want to remain in this awful place! But if she's powerful enough to entrance you and force you from your bed to follow her, do you honestly think she's going to let you escape from her?"

"I'd be out of here like a shot if you'd come with me. I won't leave you behind."

"She's already prevented you from going off the grounds, even for a few hours. Face it, Guy, we're trapped here."

"Are you trying to tell me she made the rental car malfunction?" He shook his head.

"You told me yourself the car started for the mechanic and for Rebecca but not for you."

"Even if I could accept that, what's to stop me from walking away? I almost did the other day. I would have, except when I got to the gates a feeling came over me that you were in danger. That's when I found you with the snake."

Lia gazed steadily at him. "What turned you back doesn't matter. If it hadn't been worry over me, something else would have stopped you. She won't let you go."

He sat up straight, shifting until he faced her. "I don't deny she scares me, but I'm damned if I'll agree that there's no way out."

She eased her legs from under her, pulling at the edges of her short nightgown. "Calm down. I didn't say we can't overcome her. We can but it has to be here, on her home territory."

"Yours, too, since you carry de la Roche blood."

She shook her head violently. "Not mine! The blood might be but not this haunted estate. No wonder Rebecca refused to inherit, no wonder she persuaded Aunt Marie-Louise to leave it to me."

"I'm not arguing." He spoke absently, no longer meeting her gaze. Instead he was looking at her thighs.

She glanced down, tugging again at the edge of the gown, uneasily aware it revealed a good bit of thigh.

"I'm sorry," he said. "I know it wasn't me but somehow I feel responsible."

Only then did she realize he was focusing on the large bruise that darkened her inner thigh and she flushed, not wanting to remember how she'd gotten the bruise. It hadn't been his fault. Or hers. The bruise would fade in time but she feared the memory would linger, becoming a permanent stain.

He bent his head and, before she understood his intent, he brushed his lips very gently over the bruise, not otherwise touching her. He didn't need to. The feel of his mouth on her inner thigh sent a tingling message of pleasure along her nerves, arousing her, making her ache for more.

Straightening, he ran his forefinger along the curve of her lips. She had difficulty restraining her impulse to take his finger into her mouth and suck on it.

"Do you have any idea what I'd like to do?" he asked in a husky rasp.

"Don't tell me," she said hastily. "My imagination is already overloaded. This is dangerous. We'd better start talking about something else, like the weather, in a hurry."

He leaned back, away from her. "I know, I know. But that won't cancel what I want."

She wanted it, too, wanted his mouth slanted over hers, the taste of him beguiling her senses while his hands caressed her in the way that only he could. . . .

"If you keep looking at me like that," he said, "I'm damn well going to do everything we both want."

"No, wait, I'll stop." She gazed at his feet instead of into his eyes. "Why don't you let me wash those cuts and find some antiseptic to put on them?"

"Not a good idea. Considering my present condition, if you so much as touched a single toe of mine you'd be in my arms the next second and five minutes later—"

"Okay, I get the picture—no foot washing. Um, weather. Tell me, what's your opinion of the tropical disturbance in the Gulf?"

He shrugged. "Sulie seems to have a talent for being right. It's early in the season for a full-fledged hurricane but we're probably in for a pretty good storm."

"The Dread One's kind of weather," she said. Why was it that everything led back to Evangeline? "Will you search for her grave again tomorrow?"

"That depends on whether there's time enough."

She blinked. "Why wouldn't there be?"

"What with the gardener and those clean-sweep people coming, I meant."

Though she didn't quite see why any of them would interfere, because of the sudden curtain of fatigue that had rolled down over her, she let it go, yawning.

"Ready for bed?" he asked.

"I don't want to be alone in my room," she admitted.

"I don't want to be alone in mine, either. Unfortunately, together we're dynamite with the fuse burning closer and closer."

She yawned again. "I could curl up on this couch and you could stretch out like you were before, with your feet on the stool. It wouldn't be like we were in bed together."

He raised his eyebrows. "It's news to me that we need a bed to get into trouble."

"Do you have a better solution?"

"No," he admitted, stretching his legs until his feet rested on the stool. "So, good night."

"Sleep tight," she murmured sleepily from where she curled in the corner of the couch, her eyes already shut.

He watched her for long moments before closing his eyes. Lia was lovely, courageous and the sexiest woman he'd ever met. She was also vulnerable and he'd give anything to keep her safe.

Sleep tight, she'd told him, words his mother had often used. When he was a child he'd believed that meant all wrapped in the covers, warm and snug and safe, with no bad dreams. The words were not a magic formula because the same nightmare vision that menaced him now had troubled him even then.

He wouldn't sleep, he'd merely rest. And he wouldn't dwell on what had happened to him hours earlier, he'd go back to happier days with his parents, the man and woman who'd adopted and loved him.

His father hadn't been an absentee dad, he'd always been there for the school events, always had time for a game of catch and the occasional camping trip into the Sierras. He'd had a good childhood....

When he first heard the voice, Guy thought for a moment he was a child, his father speaking to him. *Remember,* the man said, as his father so often had, signaling he was about to say something he considered important.

Remember to listen. Not his father. Nor was he a child. And the voice was in his head.

Listen. Remember what you hear. If you don't understand, you must memorize. Or die.

He listened but the voice said nothing more, leaving him with the last word echoing in his mind.

Die. Die. Die...

CHAPTER ELEVEN

Guy woke to the clang of metal on metal. His cramped muscles protested when he sat up straight—why the hell was he on the library couch? Lia blinked sleepily at him from the corner of the couch and he remembered.

"Someone's at the front door," he said.

Lia yawned. "Sulie'll answer it."

Probably the gardener, Fred Somebody, he decided, since the clean-sweep crew should know by now to use the back door. Sulie could handle the gardener, but, since the cleaning people would be here sooner or later, he and Lia needed to retreat upstairs and get dressed.

"Fred Speer, I'll bet," Lia said, uncurling. "I have to talk to him before he gets started. I want him to begin by cutting back the growth near the gazebo." She eased off the couch, slid on her slippers and and started for the library door. She paused, turned back and smiled so sweetly at Guy that his heart turned over. "Good morning."

He hid his reaction. "And a good morning to you. I hope you're not going to give poor Fred a heart attack by meeting him in that sexy shirt you sleep in."

"Heavens, no. Gardeners are too difficult to find. See you at breakfast."

By the time Guy dressed and came downstairs, the cleaning crew had arrived. He found no one in the kitchen and assumed Lia was still upstairs. He was drinking his second cup of coffee and eating the third one of Sulie's Creole doughnuts covered with powdered sugar—he couldn't remember what she called them, something beginning with *b*—when Sulie came in the back door.

"She ain't gonna like it," Sulie announced.

"Do you mean Lia?" he asked, uncertain what she was talking about.

Sulie shook her head. "*Her.* Me, I tell Miss Lia, I say don't let that man be messing with the gazebo lest she be angry. Miss Lia, she don't listen."

Guy dropped his unfinished doughnut and sprang up from the table. "Where *is* Lia?"

Sulie gestured toward the side garden. "Be by the gazebo. With that man."

He was through the door as she said the last word. He strode toward the gazebo trying to convince himself his uneasiness was ridiculous. He failed. As far as he was concerned, Lia wasn't safe anywhere on this damned estate. On top of that, he had a premonition of immediate danger—if he didn't reach her in a hurry he'd be too late.

The gardener had already widened the path to the gazebo, leaving a trail of cuttings on the ground. By the time Guy neared him, he was clipping the Carolina jasmine surrounding the gazebo. Guy couldn't see Lia but he heard her.

"Fred, you need to prune a bit more there to your left," she was saying.

Realizing she must be inside the gazebo, Guy broke into a run, vaulted up the steps, lifted her off her feet and carried her out, not pausing to put her down until he was ten feet away from the building.

Seeing Fred gaping at him, Guy shouted, "Get away from there. Hurry!"

Only then did Guy see the dead limb break free of the magnolia whose branches overhung the gazebo. He held his breath, hoping Fred would make it to safety. As the heavy limb crashed onto the gazebo roof, splintering it, the end of the branch clipped the gardener's right arm, knocking the long-handled pruning shears from his hand. The impact felled him.

Guy hurried to help the man to his feet, asking, "Are you hurt?"

Fred, blood trickling from a scratch on his cheek, grunted with pain as he supported his right arm with his left. "Either sprained my wrist or broke the dang thing," he muttered. He stared at the dead branch, then kicked the pruning shears from under the debris shed by the branch. "Best pair I got, wouldn't want to lose 'em."

Lia picked up the shears. "Come in the house and sit down," she insisted.

"Thanks, guess I will." Glancing at Guy, he said, "I owe you, mister. I'd've been knocked to Kingdom

Come if you hadn't yelled at me to get clear. Good thing you noticed what was happening—got the little lady out right sharp, you did, just in time.''

Guy realized Fred thought he'd seen or heard the limb crack off the tree before he rescued Lia. He left it at that.

In the kitchen, Fred let Lia dab the blood off his cheek but refused further help. ''I live in this parish, down the road a piece. My wife's home, it's her day off. I can get to my house driving left-handed. Being a nurse, she'll decide what to do next.''

''I'm so sorry,'' Lia said. ''Are you sure you can make it home alone?''

Fred nodded. ''Been hurt worse.''

''I'll call LaBranche about the insurance,'' Guy said.

''I'd appreciate that. You can drop those shears in my truck. Lucky I didn't unload the heavy stuff yet.''

As they walked to his truck with him, Fred said, ''Can't say when I'll be coming back. Or if. Likely Mr. LaBranche'll have to find someone else.''

''I'll tell him,'' Guy said. ''I'm sure he'll be in touch with you.''

After they watched the truck pull away, Lia asked, ''How did you know that branch was going to fall? If it had already started to break off there wouldn't have been time to rush in and grab me and get us both to safety before it came crashing down.''

''Sulie warned me,'' he said.

Her eyebrows raised. ''About the tree limb?''

He shook his head. "About upsetting the Dread One."

"Then I guess I have Sulie to thank as well as you." She raised on tiptoe and gave him a quick kiss. "You deserve more but you'll have to take a rain check."

Back in the kitchen, Sulie scolded Lia. "You got to listen when I warn you 'bout her. She don't like outsiders coming here and she don't like nobody messing with her private places. Gazebo be one, *garçonnière* be another."

"I'll listen from now on," Lia promised. "Do you think the cleaning crew is through with my room yet? I really do need to rest."

"Should be. Told 'em to do yours and his first. Best you do lay down, you be looking a tad puny." She glanced at Guy. "A nap won't be hurting you, neither. Best to take it when you can. Gonna be another long night."

Guy let Lia precede him, then said to Sulie, "If anyone comes, call me, will you?"

She gave him a shrewd look. "'Specting somebody?"

"Not exactly. I just thought maybe Maurice might drop by."

Sulie shrugged. "If he do, you'll know."

Guy no sooner hit his bed than he fell asleep. He woke with Sulie banging on his door, calling through it that Maurice was here. A glance at his watch amazed him—it was after four.

The cleaning crew was gone. He found Lia already in the morning room talking to Maurice, who was drinking coffee. She got to her feet when she saw Guy. "Look what Maurice brought to show me," she said, holding out an oval miniature of a dark-haired woman.

Guy examined the little painting. After a moment he glanced from the miniature to her and back. "It could be you," he said.

"Ask Maurice who it is."

"As I told Cousin Lia," Maurice said, "my wife reminded me about an old box of family relics left to me when Papa died. I stored the box away and more or less forgot it until Dee mentioned it. I got the box down from the crawl space above the closet, took a look at the contents and found the miniature in a case. There was a paper wrapped around the case with a name in faded ink, not my father's writing. What it said was 'Evangeline de la Roche.'"

Assessing the exquisite little painting for the second time, Guy noticed subtle differences in Evangeline's face as compared to Lia's. "She has a cruel smile," he said.

"Witch's smile," Maurice told him.

"Maybe," Guy said. "Lia's smile is not the same. Not at all."

"'Course not," Maurice said, looking at Lia. "By the way, my wife suggested I invite you and Guy to come into town and stay with us for a few days. We don't have a big house but there's a spare bedroom and a pull-out couch in the living room.

"She'd really like to meet you but, like I mentioned, she's afraid to come out here, 'specially being pregnant. She doesn't exactly believe anything here will harm the baby but she doesn't exactly not believe it, either. She won't take any chances."

"How kind of you to invite us," Lia said. "I'd love to meet your wife but—"

"Don't refuse outright," Guy said. "I think it would do us both good to get away for a few days, Lia."

"I can't argue with that, but still—"

"Dee's going to be mighty disappointed if I don't bring you two back with me," Maurice put in.

Lia bit her lip. "Let me think about it."

"Well, sure." Maurice glanced at his watch. "I can't stay much longer, though."

Guy handed the miniature back to Maurice. "Excuse us for a minute," he said. "Lia and I need to have a talk." He caught her hand and pulled her into the hall.

"I know what you're going to say," she told him in a fierce whisper, "but we can't leave."

"Let's try," he said as persuasively as he could. "You claim we can't, that she won't let us. Why don't we put it to the test? If she lets us go, that means she's not as powerful as you seem to believe, that she needs to have us on her home turf or else she can't influence us. What's the harm in trying? Either we get away free and clear or she won't let us go. We're certainly no worse off than we are now and there's a chance we'll be one hell of a lot better off. Let's take it."

She eyed him thoughtfully. "That makes sense."

"Good. We'll go up and pack. I can't wait to get out of here."

He led her upstairs, hoping she wouldn't change her mind on the way.

"I have to tell Sulie," she said, pausing at the top.

"On the way out," he told her, urging her along the hall.

Even when he carried their bags down, he was afraid Lia would decide not to go at the last instant. In the kitchen, Sulie took the news calmly.

"Go try," she said. "Be no harm to try."

He realized the old woman was certain the Dread One wouldn't let them go. He gritted his teeth, hanging grimly to his belief they'd make it.

Guy was bringing the suitcases to the car where Maurice waited when Lia, who'd been at his side, suddenly halted.

"No!" she cried. "Oh, no!" Dropping the handbag she carried, she spun around and fled into the thickness of the greenery behind the house.

By the time Guy flung down the suitcases and ran after her, she was out of sight, hidden somewhere in the overgrown tangle. He floundered through the greenery shouting her name. What the devil had spooked her? And where was she headed?

Lia didn't answer. He stopped and listened for the sound of her thrashing among the bushes. There, to his left. After what had happened in there the day before, she couldn't be going back to the *garçonnière*— not unless she was being forced to go. Apprehension gripped him. Like the smashed gazebo, the *garçonnière* had been a meeting place for the long-ago lovers and so was dangerous.

"Lia, wait!" he called.

No response. He plunged on in the direction of the *garçonnière,* following the trail of wilting branches he'd sliced off with the meat cleaver the previous day. Come to think of it, he hadn't brought the cleaver back to the house. Where had he left it? He couldn't recall.

He sighted the circle of oaks rising above the wild growth surrounding him and pushed on, finally spotting the faded white of the *garçonnière*. Increasing his pace, he reached the shadows under the trees where he paused to stare in confusion. The building before him was roofless, the octagonal sides caving in.

Close up, he saw the door gaping wide, disclosing a jumble of splintered wood and roofing slates blocking the entrance. For an instant he was horror-stricken, imagining Lia buried in the rubble. Reason came to his rescue. He would have heard the noise if the roof had collapsed in the past fifteen or twenty minutes. There'd been no crash since Lia had run into the jungle, therefore the building had fallen in on itself sometime after they'd left it yesterday but before she'd fled.

He took a deep breath and let it out in a rush of relief only to realize that he still hadn't found her. In the distance he heard a car motor, the sound growing fainter and fainter. No doubt Maurice driving off. Damn! There went the chance to get away.

"Lia!" he shouted, again and again. The darkness under the oaks swallowed her name.

"Where the hell are you?" he muttered in mingled fear and frustration.

He pivoted in a slow circle, not certain which way to go. A flicker of white caught his eye. Lia was wearing a white shirt. He stopped, peered intently at the flicker, then his shoulders slumped in disappointment. Nothing but a swarm of those damn white moths. They fluttered toward him only to veer off, angling to his left, away from the direction of the house.

About to ignore the moths, he shook his head. What were the words Sulie had used to describe them? *White magic,* yes, that was it. He'd dismissed nearly everything she'd said as superstition but what if all of it wasn't? He'd asked out loud where Lia was—and the moths had appeared. A sign? With no other clue, he might as well follow where they led. What did he have to lose?

Feeling like an idiot, he trailed after the moths, telling himself he was wasting time, that Lia had likely backtracked and returned to the house. Still, he persisted, keeping them in view as he hurried through the shadowed oak grove.

He stepped out from under the gloom of the trees, blinking in the light, reminded that it wasn't dusk, merely late afternoon. For a moment he thought he'd lost the moths but then he saw they'd descended and were settling into tall bushes not far beyond where he stood. Shrugging, he pushed on, only to notice with surprise that someone had hacked off branches to make a rough path.

Guy stopped to think it over. He hadn't come this far before. Fred, the gardener, hadn't been anywhere except near the gazebo. Unease prickled the hair on his nape. Whose path was he following? If he threw logic to the winds, it had to be Lia because she's the one the moths would lead him to. He supposed she could have found the meat cleaver—he must have left it somewhere near the *garçonnière*.

But if it *was* Lia, where was she going? If she'd reached the oaks, she couldn't be lost because the branches he'd cut yesterday left a clear trail from the oaks back to the house. This was a new trail leading God knows where. Why would she have made it? Surely she must have returned to the house by now.

He opened his mouth to call to her, then shook his head, deciding it might be prudent not to warn anyone of his presence. Moving as quietly as he could, he made his way along the path. In a few moments, four or five moths fluttered from among the bushes to either side and he knew he'd reached the spot where

they'd settled. A few more steps and something pink-
ish white showed through the greenery, a stone of
some kind.

Guy paused, parted branches to get a better view
and found himself looking at a square marble crypt
some five feet high. On the ground beside the crypt,
Lia lay huddled, the meat cleaver beside her.

He thrust himself through the branches, calling her
name. She grasped the cleaver and sprang up, her face
contorted with fear.

"Lia!" he cried.

She took a step back, brandishing the cleaver.

He stopped, puzzled. "What's wrong?" he demanded.

"How do I know who you are?" she asked.

He thought he understood. "It's all right—I'm Guy.
Me. Myself. Not the other."

She narrowed her eyes. "How do I know?"

"For one thing I called you Lia. *He* wouldn't."

She bit her lip. "I can't be sure he hasn't learned my
name."

Guy tried to think of something that might convince her, something totally unrelated to the de la
Roches or the Revenirs or New Orleans. "The City
Hall in Oakland," he said at last, "which you can see
from my office window, has a very fancy wedding cake
cupola. The building's cornerstone was laid by President Taft in 1911. Shall I go on?"

Lia dropped the cleaver and ran to him and he
wrapped his arms around her, holding her, silently

offering comfort. He longed to tell her she was safe with him and that everything would be all right, but it would be a lie.

After a time, she pulled away and he let her go. "I found the grave," she said.

"So I see." He spoke carefully, not wanting to upset her with questions.

"There's her name—Evangeline Marie-Louise de la Roche. But no date of birth. Or death." Pointing to double bronze doors in the pink marble crypt, she added in a whisper, "She's inside there."

Guy pulled away the vines twining over the bronze doors to take a closer look. He saw they were embellished with griffins, noting the rusted chain through the handles of the doors. He started when he glanced at the padlock hanging unhooked on the chain. "The damn thing's unlocked!" he blurted.

Lia gasped and edged closer to him. "I think she led me here." Her voice was so low he could hardly hear her words. "Something did, anyway."

"Moths, in my case," he muttered absently, his attention fixed on the chain and padlock.

Lia touched his arm. "Let's not stay here."

He glanced at her and decided to risk the question burning in his mind. "Tell me why you ran away instead of going with Maurice."

"When I started toward the car, she put a picture in my mind, an image of a baby inside its mother and then she—she spoiled the baby."

"Spoiled it? What's that mean?"

"The baby was normal at first but she changed it to a kind of monster." Lia grimaced, shuddering. "A creature, not a human. Oh, Guy it was so awful. I understood she was warning me that if I left the estate she'd come with me and do those horrible things to Maurice and Dee's baby. After that I couldn't go, I wouldn't go with Maurice. I was so devastated I didn't know what I was doing. All I could think of was to get away."

He gave her a quick hug, reluctant to release her but afraid to prolong the contact. "I can't blame you. But why choose the *garçonnière?*"

"It wasn't deliberate. I was frightened when I realized where I'd gotten to, the more so when I found the place in complete ruin. I wondered if I remembered wrong about entering the *garçonnière* yesterday. But then I decided she'd destroyed it the way she did the gazebo. And then I noticed the cleaver on the ground and something told me to come this way and I found the grave."

Above her head, he saw four white moths and reached up to brush them away so they wouldn't get tangled in her hair and upset her. The moths swerved away from his hand, fluttered toward the crypt and settled onto the chain holding the bronze doors closed. He frowned, staring at them.

"What are you looking at?" Lia asked, following his gaze. "Ugh, those white moths again."

"You were led here," he said, "and so was I. Not merely to look at the crypt but for some other reason. I think I've discovered that reason."

"What is it?"

"We're supposed to open those bronze doors."

She gaped at him. "Are you crazy?"

He didn't reply. Uncertain he was taking the right action but feeling compelled to take a look inside, he stepped closer and reached for the padlock.

"No! Don't!" Lia cried.

He paid no attention. Lifting the padlock from the links in the chain, he freed the two ends of the chain. It rattled against the bronze doors as he pulled it from the two handles. Rust flaked off onto the vines, leaving behind a faint metallic odor. Insects that had been chirring around them fell silent as he gripped the two handles and yanked. The doors creaked open. He'd thought he was prepared to face whatever dwelt inside but in no way had he expected what he did see.

He turned to Lia to find she'd covered her eyes with her hands. "You needn't be afraid to look," he said. "The crypt is empty."

CHAPTER TWELVE

"Me, I never say she be *in* the grave," Sulie insisted, arms akimbo as she faced Guy and Lia in the mansion's kitchen.

"But you did tell us it was Evangeline's grave," Guy said.

Sulie's hand clutched at the neck of her dress. "It be hers, all right, only she don't be buried there, don't be buried nowhere. Ole Miss say that one's papa, he put up the crypt for what they call a monument."

"If Evangeline isn't buried anywhere, where is she?" Lia asked.

Sulie changed position, sliding her hands up her arms as though she had a chill. "Her bones be on the bottom of the bayou, that's where they be. More'n a hundred years ago she drowned in that bayou in a bad storm and they never find her. But her, she don't stay dead, she come back and be the Dread One. 'Cause she died in a storm she got the power to call up storms. Like the one we gonna get." She jerked her head toward the radio. "Weatherman, he say that tropical disturbance be gaining power, be coming this way."

"How soon?" Guy asked, crossing to turn on the radio.

"He say he don't know yet. Me, I say it be tomorrow night and it be a bad one."

Lia left Guy fiddling with the radio and followed Sulie into the pantry. "I hope Maurice wasn't angry with me," she said in a low tone.

"He be a de la Roche so deep down he knows you ain't gonna leave this place easy. He ask me what happen, I say Miss Lia can't go, Mr. Guy, neither. I tell him to carry the bags upstairs before he drive his car away."

"I would have gone with Maurice but she—"

Sulie held up her hand. "Don't make no difference how she stop you. Me, I know she don't let you go. When the moon rise tonight, after Mr. Guy be sleeping, me, I help you learn what to do."

Lia nodded, feeling a flutter of power within. She desperately needed to learn how to use what she had. And it was best Guy be asleep when she did because he wouldn't understand and might try to stop her.

She leaned closer to Sulie, lowering her voice even more. "There's a problem. She gets into his dreams. We can't let that happen tonight."

"Gris-gris maybe keep her away from him long enough for you to learn how to use fire."

Lia wasn't too confident. Although, come to think of it, Sulie had put a gris-gris by her bed the first night she was in the house and she'd been safe enough in her bedroom. Maybe it would work in Guy's bedroom as well.

As if evoked, Guy appeared in the pantry doorway. "We may actually get a hurricane by tomorrow night," he said. "They've named it, which means they're taking the storm seriously. You'll never guess the name they chose."

"Give me a hint."

"It's not Rumpelstiltskin."

"How could it be? This is a woman's name year, not a man's."

"Okay, it's not Xanthippe, either."

"We aren't that many storms into the alphabet."

He grinned at her. "Try Ophelia and you've got it. I'd say that puts the storm on our side, right?"

"Praise the Lord, it's a sign," Sulie said softly. "The first sign."

Ophelia. The word echoed in Lia's mind. Though she didn't use the name, it was her real name. Her true name. Was it a good omen, as Sulie believed? Even Guy seemed elated.

"Gonna make you a gris-gris," Sulie told Guy. "Me, I hang it on your bed and you don't touch that gris-gris, you hear? It help keep her away tonight."

"A gris-gris is a kind of amulet," Lia put in.

Guy shrugged. "It can't hurt, that's for sure. A man in a New Orleans shop tried to sell me an amulet, maybe it was a gris-gris. He said something about St. John's root, whatever that is."

Sulie shook her head. "You don't never want to be messing with St. John's root. Must be that man had a voodoo shop."

"Could be. He had something rather odd as a window display, a large twisted root—mandrake, he said. He claimed people saw illusions in the twists and turns of the root. As I recall, he saw someone he called Damballah, returning to rule the earth."

"Voodoo for sure," Sulie muttered.

"Did you see anything?" Lia asked.

Guy shifted his shoulders. "I'm not sure. I thought for a moment I saw a man and woman tangled together in the same way the roots were, so intertwined one couldn't be separated from the other."

"Who were they?" Lia persisted.

He shrugged, giving her the feeling he was deliberately evading an answer.

"You be seeing true," Sulie told him. "Those two from the past be linked same like a chain, got to break the links, you and Miss Lia, lest you both be chained with them."

Guy fixed his gaze on Sulie. "You'd be more help if you told us the entire story instead of feeding us cryptic bits and pieces. Never mind what you promised Ole Miss. Marie-Louise de la Roche is dead but we're alive and we'd like to stay that way."

"Me, I want to stay alive, too," Sulie said. "Seem to me I tell too much already." She pushed past him, crossed the kitchen to the back stairs and disappeared from sight.

"Isn't that called coercing a witness?" Lia asked.

He smiled wryly. "No, merely attempting to. Sulie's not easily coercible. What's this gris-gris she means to hang on my bed?"

"A revolting combination of feathers and bones and other unlikely objects. She put one in my room and I have to admit nothing terrible has happened to me there."

"As long as it's not alive. We have enough problems without strange animals loose in the house."

"There haven't been any live animals in this house for a long time. Sulie says cats wouldn't stay here and that Aunt Marie-Louise refused to get another dog after her little terrier disappeared. Sulie thinks the Dread One lured the dog to the bayou and fed him to an alligator to get even with Marie-Louise for preventing her from using her power."

"Sulie's hinted often enough that Ole Miss could control the Dread One. I wonder how." He looked at Lia. "You don't really go along with Sulie's notion that you have power and must learn to use it—or do you?"

"I won't know until I try." Lia deliberately hedged, hoping she wouldn't be forced to lie to Guy to keep him from interfering tonight.

"Moonlight and fire, right?"

"So Sulie says."

"Then you may have to wait," Guy said. "The weatherman predicts a cloud cover this evening, a harbinger of the coming storm."

* * *

Midnight passed before Lia could be certain Guy slept. Earlier, clouds did arrive and they still covered the moon so she was certain he didn't suspect she meant to leave the house, but she was taking no chances.

She crept from her room, being careful to make no noise since his door stood open, and slipped down the back stairs. Sulie waited for her by the kitchen door and, when she saw Lia, she eased through the door into the cloudy night. As Lia followed, the moon broke through the cloud cover.

"The second sign for us," Sulie said softly. "Moonlight shows the way."

Lia wore a short white silk robe Sulie had given her and nothing else except her slippers. As they hurried through the greenery toward the cleared circle where she'd met Kos, the night sounds gradually faded from her consciousness until all she heard was the thrum of power beating within her.

When they reached the clearing, Sulie, wearing a long blue gown and a blue turban she called a *tignon*, set down the basket she'd been carrying and removed its contents, setting everything out.

"Make the fire ready," she ordered. Seating herself cross-legged on the ground, she began tapping her fingers on a small drum.

Lia, knowing she must do everything herself, arranged the small white rocks in a circle, propped the kindling into a pyramid around wood shavings, struck a long, white match and touched its brief flare to the shavings. The shavings caught and tiny flames began licking at the dry wood. With the kindling well aflame, she added larger sticks until the small fire burned steadily.

She kicked off her slippers, untied the robe and shrugged it off. "Kos," she murmured. "Come to me, Kos, for I am Ophelia. Come to the fire."

Though she was no longer fully aware of her surroundings, she knew the soft rhythm of the drum matched the beat of her heart. She sensed Kos before she saw his blackness weave between the fire and where she stood.

Bending down, she lifted the snake until he draped her shoulders. When she held out her left arm, he laid his head on the palm of her hand. Slowly, keeping time to the beat of the drum, she began to circle the fire sunwise, dancing the way of the light as opposed to the other direction, the way of the dark.

Her power came from the light, from the moon, it rose from the flames through Kos, who, as he channeled the power, magnified it before transmitting the strength that dwelt within the light to her. She knew this in the same way that she knew her true name. Both had been given to her at birth but had lain dormant. She'd never used her name nor her power because she'd never needed either. Until now.

As the rhythm of the drum increased, so did her dance, her heart pounding in time to the frantic beats.

Sunwise, lightwise, she circled with Kos, his tongue flicking rapidly, absorbing power from the flames.

Guy woke slowly, shaking off the shards of a dream that he couldn't quite remember, not an unpleasant dream, something to do with fire. He lay quietly, childhood memories of campfires filling him with nostalgia. How he'd enjoyed those trips to the mountains with his father. With Bradford Russell, the man who'd been his real father, though not his birth father.

His uncles had been right—he should have left well enough alone. But could he have? He shook his head. The woman in white would have drawn him here no matter what.

"Damn you!" he said aloud. "I'm only a Revenir by accident."

Now fully awake and thirsty, he rose, noticing the swathe of moonlight slanting through his window. The sky must have cleared. He pulled on his pajama pants and thrust his feet into his moccasins before leaving the room. If she could see him, he thought with a half smile, Sulie would scold him for deserting the protection of her gris-gris.

In the kitchen, he paused on his way to the refrigerator, frowning at the open back door. Sulie locked up every night. Who'd gone out? Remembering the moonlight, he cursed, turned on his heel, vaulted up the back stairs and flung himself into Lia's room. Her bed was empty, the room was empty.

He'd bet his last dollar Sulie wasn't in her bed, either. They were under the moon somewhere on the grounds with a fire of their own. But not a campfire, a fire to call up power. And snakes as well, for all he knew.

Where? Reminded of the clearing where he'd discovered Lia holding that damn blacksnake, Guy raced down the stairs and out the back door. Didn't Lia realize the danger she exposed herself to? Not from mumbo jumbo chanted by a fire and not even from snakes. Far worse than snakes stalked these grounds at night.

Moonlight showed him the path to the clearing. As he pushed his way through the growth, the night's silence was split by a reverberating roar that stopped him momentarily. He'd never heard anything like that terrifying bellow. An animal—but what kind of animal? And where the devil was it?

"Lia!" he shouted, plunging on.

He'd almost reached the clearing when Sulie's thin figure stepped in front of him. "You don't go near her," she warned. When Guy tried to push past her, she caught his arm, her fingernails digging into his flesh. "No. Leave her be lest you harm her."

"That roaring," he said. "What—?"

"Be a bull gator in the swamp beyond the bayou. He be calling his mate, he don't be bothering us."

Looking past Sulie he caught a glimpse of a woman's figure outlined against a dying fire. Lia. She wore some kind of robe that humped up over her shoulders. No, not a robe, he realized in horror. What was draped over her shoulders was that damn snake.

Sulie's grip on his arm tightened. "Kos won't harm her," she said as though reading his mind. "He be helping her gain power. Wait."

"The hell I'll wait," he muttered, trying to shake her off.

"You be Revenir or you be your own self?" she demanded.

Her question took him aback. "Myself!" he snapped.

"Promise you do what I say before you go to Miss Lia."

She clung to him like a burr. Either he promised or he'd have to drag her with him into the clearing. "What is it you want?"

"You don't be touching her, don't be calling to her. Just stand and watch till the fire goes dark. Kos, he leave then and she be herself."

An icy chill trickled along his spine. "Who is she now?"

"Not *her*. Still be Miss Lia, only she be someplace else. Harm come do you break the spell."

Guy decided that Lia must be in some kind of trance. Apprehensive as he was, he knew enough to understand she shouldn't be shocked from the trance but allowed to come out of it in her own way.

"I'll do as you tell me," he muttered. "But in return, I expect you to tell us all you know about—" He broke off, sensing a danger in speaking names aloud at this time in this place. "All you know about them, about those two from the past," he finished.

"Ole Miss—" Sulie began.

He cut her off. "Is it a bargain or not?"

She nodded slowly and let him go, trailing after him as he entered the clearing and approached the fire. Only a few feeble flames licked at the burnt wood. He stopped near Lia, close enough to reach her quickly if she needed him. Sulie came up beside him.

Despite his unease at what was going on, Guy couldn't help but admire the beauty of Lia's body—she was the loveliest woman he'd ever seen. No man could look at her and not want her. Yet what he felt for her was more than simple lust, more complex than desire. He wanted her, yes, but for all time.

Intent on the last flickering flames, she didn't appear to notice either him or Sulie. The snake, its head resting on her outstretched left palm, also watched the fire.

When the last flame wavered and died, Lia brought her left hand toward her face. As the snake's quivering, forked tongue neared her lips, Guy tensed, taking an involuntary step forward.

"Power comes to them who be kissed by a snake," Sulie whispered in his ear.

Reminding himself that blacksnakes were, in fact, not poisonous, he gritted his teeth and forced himself not to move.

The snake's tongue touched Lia's lips, then its head drew back. Kneeling, Lia lifted its body from her shoulders to the ground and the snake undulated rapidly away. When she rose, Sulie hurried to her and draped a white robe over her shoulders. As Lia slid her arms into the robe, she looked around, her expression dazed. She saw Guy and blinked, then hurriedly drew the robe closed and tied the belt.

He found himself with nothing to say. All he could do was gaze into her dark eyes, losing himself in their depths. They stood facing each other, not touching until a loud splash from the bayou startled them both.

Sulie, who'd been replacing the white stones in the basket, cried, "The Dread One, she be sending that gator after me just like she do with that little dog."

"Let's get the hell back to the house," Guy said, clasping Lia's hand. "Come on, Sulie, leave that stuff."

Sulie didn't move. "Won't do no good to run, gator gonna get me no matter what."

"No!" Lia pulled free of Guy and ran, not toward the house but toward the bayou.

He pounded after her, calling, "Come back!"

When he caught up to her she was standing near the bank of the bayou facing a huge alligator that was pulling itself from the black water. She pointed her right forefinger at the monster and lifted her left hand, palm toward it. "I am Ophelia," she said. "I say, No."

Guy lunged for her, hoping he could pull her to safety before the gator grabbed her. But he saw, as he was hauling her backward, that, instead of attacking, the animal was retreating, sliding down until the dark water covered it completely.

Sulie stood beside them, staring at the bayou. "The third sign," she whispered. "You be stronger'n Ole Miss."

No one said another word until they reached the house. In the kitchen, after Sulie brewed a fresh pot of coffee, the three of them sat at the kitchen table.

"Me, I promise to tell him what Ole Miss knew," Sulie said, "and the Dread One, she don't be wanting you to know so she send that gator to kill me."

Guy still hadn't assimilated what he'd seen at the bayou. Had Lia actually turned that alligator back or was it a lucky coincidence that the beast decided to retreat at that particular moment? But why had the gator left the swamp and come to the grounds in the first place? Another coincidence?

Uncle Tim always used to say that it was permissible for an attorney to accept one coincidence but never two.

Did Lia actually have some psychic power?

Sulie took a long swallow of coffee and set her cup down. "Ole Miss burn all those family papers 'cause she don't be wanting anybody to read about Miss Evangeline." As she said the name, Guy saw Sulie's hand go to her neck as though to touch some amulet hidden by her high-necked gown.

"Ole Miss tell me there don't be no witness to what happen that night, only the two of them, the two from the past. She say after that night, the de la Roche family never speak again to the Revenir family.''

"But did she tell you what she thought happened?'' Guy asked.

Sulie nodded. "She read all them papers and she say it be murder, not drowning.''

Guy thought of the slashed painting and the rusty stains on the chaise longue and the carpet in the *garçonnière*. Old bloodstains?

"Everybody think Miss Evangeline, she drown in the bayou. The same night Mr. Revenir, he disappear. Whatever happen, wherever he go he be leaving his wife and sons behind and don't ever come back.''

"How can they be sure that he didn't drown, too?'' Lia asked.

"'Cause the de la Roche stableboy, he be there when Mr. Revenir come after his horse. Boy say he hollering and moaning about somebody drowning. Horse and man, they ride off in the storm. Revenirs be living in this same parish then, down the road. Him, he get the horse home—his stableman see him—but he never go in his house.''

"And no one ever saw him again?'' Lia asked.

"They be claiming they don't. Ole Miss, she think he kill Miss Evangeline and throw her in the bayou. She say that's why he run away and that's why Miss Evangeline, she can't rest, always be searching for him so she can avenge her murder.

"She change to the Dread One, be luring men to her, be taking them with her to the bottom of the bayou to lie with her bones. Long time this be happening, till Ole Miss be born, grow up and find she got enough power to stop the Dread One—but then she die and the Dread One, she come back and she keep searching.''

Sulie fixed her gaze on Guy. ''She finally be finding a Revenir. Then she need to get him here. Miss Rebecca, she be too old, no good for that. The Dread One, she go looking for a pretty one, a young de la Roche woman to use and she find Miss Lia.

''Ole Miss, she get too feeble to be warding off the Dread One. So the Dread One, she be putting it in Ole Miss's mind to leave the place to Miss Lia so the Revenir can be lured here. The Dread One, she be searching long and long. Now she got you and she ain't never gonna let you go.''

Guy glanced at Lia, who was staring intently at Sulie. ''Murder,'' she said slowly. ''Vengeance.''

She almost seemed to relish the words, making him uneasy. It wasn't like Lia. All at once he wondered if she really *was* Lia. He might be able to accept that the woman who'd turned the gator aside had power, but how could he be positive who that woman was?

Was she Lia, who'd supposedly acquired power from fire and snakes? Or was she the one who'd already proven her tremendous power?

Was she Evangeline?

CHAPTER THIRTEEN

Sulie got up from the kitchen table. "Me, I got old bones," she said. "Old bones, they need rest." She looked from Lia to Guy. "Best you both stay close to them gris-gris, you hear? Don't know how much good they be doing but they be the only protection you got."

Lia nodded absently, murmuring, "Good night," as Sulie left the room. She was bothered by the way Guy was looking at her. Why did he stare so intently? Glancing down she noticed that the V of the silk robe showed more cleavage than she'd meant to reveal and she pulled the sides closer together.

He smiled slightly. "Aren't you going to take her advice?"

Though Lia felt tired, she wasn't sleepy. "Soon," she said, reluctant to go to her room. She would be alone there and she didn't want to be alone.

"Soon." He repeated the word, she decided, as though searching for some hidden significance. "Why not now? I should think you'd be exhausted."

Why was he nagging her? "What's with you?" she demanded, tartness creeping into her voice. "Don't you believe I'm capable of making my own decision about whether or not to go to bed?"

"That depends."

She waited for more but he didn't add anything else, so she prodded him. "Depends on what?"

"On who's in charge."

"That doesn't make any sense whatsoever!"

He rose, pushing his chair back, and stood over her. "I can't be sure anymore who the hell you are."

She gazed up at him incredulously. "I'm Lia—how could you possibly believe otherwise? Didn't you hear what Sulie said about the early de la Roches speaking only French? If I was the other I'd be talking in French, wouldn't I?"

"I don't know. Evangeline may have spoken no English while she lived but does that mean, powerful as she is now, that she still can't?"

Feeling oppressed by the way he loomed over her, Lia got to her feet. "Then why does she speak only French in your dreams? *Je reviens* certainly isn't English."

The French words seemed to hang in the air between them, their English meaning echoing in her mind. *I return. I return. . . .*

Guy blinked and shook his head, muttering, "No." His voice rose. "No!"

A moment later Lia realized what he was protesting but her understanding came too late for her to fight her own invasion.

Slanting a smile at him, she loosened the sash of her silk robe so the curve of her breasts showed in the deepened V. His yellow cat's eyes glowed as his gaze took in the view. He reached for her with lazy assurance and she laughed, spun away and ran to the door, calling over her shoulder, *"Au revoir."*

"Sorcière!" he accused, chasing her through the door and into the moonlit night.

She delighted in the game of pursuit, playing catch-me-if-you-can added a special zest to what came afterward. Ah, how marvelous what would happen when at last he captured her. No man equaled him, or ever could. He'd spoiled her for any other.

She fled from him through the tangled growth, selecting her goal. Not the gazebo nor the *garçonnière*, she wanted no roof over her head, no roof other than the dark, star-sprinkled arch of the heavens.

The moon was full but low, setting, its silver light casting a moonglade along the bayou, beautiful but not her path tonight. Her path must be chosen at random, making it more difficult for him, for he'd have no clue to where she was going. How angry he'd be! Ah, but anger heated the blood and so their lovemaking would be all the hotter, blazing like a comet in the night.

Tonight she must tell him—but, no, she wouldn't think of that yet, not when there was the chase to enjoy and then the ecstasy of the capture. Already she sensed desire coiling within her, waiting for his touch to spring fiercely free.

She reveled in her assurance he'd follow her anywhere. Hadn't he insisted again and again that she'd ensorcelled him? That her lips, her body cast a spell no man could resist? Perhaps it was as well he didn't seem to understand that she was as enmeshed as he was, that she could no more break free than he could.

Her pace slowed as she came out from under the shelter of the oaks. Where now? A path beckoned and she followed it, pausing when it came to an end. Here, then. She untied the sash so her robe hung open, her heart pounding with anticipation as she waited for him to find her.

She was indeed a *sorcière,* a witch, he told himself as he raced after her. She had an uncanny ability to leave a trail of scent, her own, tempting and unforgettable, mixed with the sweetness of jasmine, a trail he could follow with his eyes closed if he had to.

He detested this game she played and yet chasing her made him all the more avid when he caught her. It had to do, he'd decided, with hunter and prey, and at first he'd believed he was the victorious hunter. Lately, he wasn't so certain of this, for didn't the hunter eventually consume his prey? Never mind who chased whom, he'd begun to suspect he was the one being consumed.

He'd realized immediately she wasn't heading for the gazebo. Her destination seemed to be the *garçonnière* but he soon discovered she'd passed it by and continued on through the oak grove. He'd never liked these oaks with their branches dripping gray moss tears and he scowled as he followed her scent between the dark trees. Where was she going?

He had no more sense, he told himself, than that of a dumb animal being lured to destruction. If he had any will, he'd turn on his heel and go home. Home was where he should be. Where he belonged, instead of wandering over the de la Roche grounds, following her, as driven as any cur panting after a bitch in heat.

If only he could conquer this fiery, demanding need for her. Each time they made love his desire seemed to increase rather than wane, as it should do. She was a fever in his blood, one that no medicine could cure.

If what he felt for her was love, it wasn't God-given but belonged to the devil.

When at last he was free of the oaks, the feeble light of the setting moon showed him a path. He strode along it, anger rising with his desire until he ached with the need to punish as well as make love.

She heard him approach and deliberately turned her back, poised to slip off her robe, then perversely decided to leave it on. She knew he'd reached the end of the path and that he saw her but she kept her back to him, waiting, saying nothing.

He didn't speak, either. And, for a long moment, he didn't move. She shifted slightly, allowing the robe to slip off one shoulder.

She felt rather than heard him close the gap between them, then he gathered her against him, her back to his front. The feel of his arousal excited her and she wriggled her hips against him, making him draw in his breath. He cupped his hands around her bare breasts, his thumbs flicking over her erect nipples until she was overcome with need and tried to turn in his arms.

He refused to allow it, keeping one hand at her breast while his other hand eased along her stomach, down and down until his fingers slipped inside her. She cried out, gasping, writhing, burning with exquisite agony.

He flung her onto the ground, tore open his breeches, dropped down and rammed into her, thrusting hard and fast. She screamed, wrapping her arms and legs about him while a wild, pulsing pleasure gripped her.

Afterward he rolled off and lay on his back, not touching her. Though she longed to feel cherished, that was not his way and he refused to change. No woman would ever truly tame him and her awareness of this was one of the reasons she'd been drawn to him in the beginning. No, he couldn't be tamed but he could be aroused.

Her lips curved into a secret smile—a cruel smile, he'd once called it—and she rose, stretched sinuously and began to dance under the light of the stars, for the moon was down. Her dance had no name. She'd learned this dance as a child by creeping from the house at night and spying on the slaves who held clandestine voodoo ceremonies near the swamp.

She'd watched how the women lured the men to them with their dancing, carefully noting which dancer the men competed for and how that dancer moved her body. What happened afterward had heated her blood, young as she was, making her yearn to be old enough to have a man of her own.

She circled him, twisting, turning, bending her body. At first he paid little attention but when she straddled him, one foot on either side of his body, raised her arms to the heavens and undulated her hips in the way she'd learned from from the voodoo dancer, she heard his breath quicken. His hands grasped her ankles.

Easing down, she brushed herself back and forth across the part of him that had quickened like his breathing. He groaned, slid his hands up to her waist and pulled her onto him until she was impaled. Closing her eyes, she threw back her head and rode him hot and hard, pleasuring herself, delighting in his hoarse gasps of passion, bringing both of them to the precipice and over.

She collapsed onto him, temporarily spent, savoring the feel of his warm body under hers. But as she'd expected, she wasn't allowed to remain where she was. Almost immediately he eased her up and off him until they were no longer touching.

Reluctant to abandon the closeness, she raised herself, leaned over and kissed him. He turned his face from her. Hurt and anger seethed in her heart. She hated his indifference afterward. Why must he push her away?

She'd meant to approach the matter delicately, choosing just the right moment but his coldness drove her to bluntness. *"Je suis enciente,"* she told him.

He sat up abruptly. *"Quoi?"* He sounded incredulous.

She repeated her words, going on to insist that because she was with child he must divorce his wife and marry her. Wasn't that what they both wished for?

Clouds slid over the stars so that darkness hid his expression but she sensed his rage and edged away. She was too late. He gripped her shoulders, shaking her so hard her teeth rattled.

"Arrêtez!" she cried, frightened by his violence.

He stopped, but only to fasten his hands around her throat instead while he reviled her, accusing her of sorcery. Choking and gasping, she managed to wrench away from him, spring to her feet and flee, naked, paying no heed to where she was going.

Hearing him in pursuit, she ran in blind fright, her only thought to get away. When her bare feet sank into the mire she realized she'd reached the edge of the bayou. She stopped so suddenly that she lost her balance and screamed as she felt herself falling.

Strong hands gripped her arm but, instead of being pulled to safety, she found herself dangling over the water. He meant to kill her!

Half-mad with rage, he could think of nothing he would rather do than choke the life from this devious little bitch who'd led him into such a trap. Divorce his wife? Never! But he saw no way to prevent a scandal that would ruin him. Unless the witch were to die.

She was at his mercy, the bayou at hand and he knew she couldn't swim....

Quel est vôtre nom? He started, almost losing his hold on her arm, then realized the voice was in his head, a man's voice speaking in his head. He almost understood the words before their meaning slipped away and was lost.

Pardon, I forgot, the voice said. *What is your name?*

"Guy," he said slowly. "Guy Russell."

Only then did he realize where he was—balanced on the edge of the bayou with a precarious grip on Lia's arm. He yanked her toward him with such force he toppled backward into the muck with Lia on top of him.

Aghast at their narrow escape, he hugged her to him. She struggled, crying, "Let me go!" And then with a surge of horror he remembered everything that had happened.

As soon as he released her, Lia scrambled to her feet. He got up more slowly. "Don't touch me!" she ordered. "I don't care if you are Guy Russell now—don't come anywhere near me."

He didn't blame her. On the other hand, they couldn't remain here by the bayou naked and covered with muck. "Sorry," he said, "but it's so dark we'll have to hold hands to avoid losing each other on our way back to the house."

After a long moment, her hand crept into his. He quelled his urge to try to comfort her—this definitely wasn't the time or the place.

They groped through the darkness in silence until Guy stumbled against what he thought was a rock and discovered they were at the crypt. At the same time, Lia cried, "I've found one of my slippers."

Searching the ground with their hands, they retrieved her robe and his pajama bottoms and moccasins. He thought the grave site was a strange place to choose for making love, if the violent passion between the others could be called that.

"You tried to kill me," Lia accused as they went on.

"Not me, you know that. *He* tried to kill *her.*"

Lia was silent for a time. " *'Enciente.'* But did he actually push her into the bayou?" she asked at last.

"He wanted to," Guy said grimly.

"Still, we don't know that's what actually happened, although Aunt Marie-Louise told Sulie that she *did* drown."

"And that he disappeared not long afterward," Guy added.

Another silence ensued, finally broken by Lia. "It won't be over and done with and we won't be free until we discover exactly what took place that night."

They'd learned at least part of what had occurred long ago by involuntarily reliving the past. He winced when he thought of what he'd done to Lia. No, damn it, he hadn't, the other was responsible. And she hadn't been Lia at the time. Unfortunately, she'd be able to recall every detail of what had happened between them, just as he did.

He hoped the memory wouldn't embed itself in her mind and fester like a splinter.

As soon as they reached the house, Lia rushed up the back stairs and into the shower. Hot water and soap couldn't remove the knowledge of what she'd been forced to do by the other but at least she was able to wash the mud from her skin and hair. The promise of dawn lightened the overcast sky by the time she finished and she found Sulie waiting in her bedroom.

"Never you mind," the old woman said after Lia had poured forth her distress and outrage at what she'd been forced to do. "You listen to me, you do like I say and maybe that be the last time she take you over."

"Are you sure? If the power Kos transferred to me from the fire didn't stop her, what will?"

"That storm she called up be coming. She think the storm be giving her more power but she be wrong. Them weather folk don't be naming the storm Ophelia for no reason. That storm got your name, it be your storm to use, not hers."

"Even if it is named for me," Lia said doubtfully, "I don't know how to go about harnessing power from a storm."

"You be learning, you got no choice. 'Course you got to be out in the storm to learn."

Lia sighed and glanced from the window at the clouded sky. "Whatever is to happen, I'd better try to get some sleep before it hits."

Sulie nodded. "Me, I make sure Mr. Guy don't be getting in your way." She turned and left the room.

Easing onto the bed, Lia wondered why Sulie would believe Guy might get in her way while she slept when very likely he'd be sprawled on his own bed asleep. It didn't make sense—but then Sulie didn't always. She shrugged and closed her eyes, only to see in her mind the image of herself being forced to dance naked under the stars, straddling Guy's body and . . .

No! She refused to remember. But she found that was easier said than done. When all else failed, she managed to dredge up a litany of abbreviations of Latin terms she'd had to learn when she was taking the medical librarian's course in Oakland.

"A.C.," she chanted under her breath, "*Ante Cibum,* before meals. P.C., *Post Cibum,* after meals." She'd reached H.S., *Hora Somni,* hour of sleep, when she felt herself drifting off.

As sleep enfolded her, it occurred to Lia that when Sulie offered to keep Guy from getting in her way, she'd meant some other time, not here and now. She was too drowsy to take the thought any further.

When in midafternoon the combination of the rising wind and the feeling she was being watched woke her, Lia had forgotten Sulie's comment. She started when she saw Guy closing her windows.

"Oh!"

He glanced at her, saying, "I didn't mean to wake you. Sulie sent me upstairs to shut the windows before the rain begins. She said they used to fasten the shutters, too, but of those that remain, most of them no longer work.''

Keeping a wary eye on him, Lia sat up, wishing she'd chosen to put on something more than briefs and a long T-shirt.

''You realize we're trapped here until the storm's over,'' he told her.

She grimaced. ''We were trapped here long before the storm was even a minor tropical disturbance.''

He closed the last of her windows and turned toward her. She tensed. Evidently noticing, he shook his head. ''It's me, not the other. You have nothing to worry about.''

''At the moment,'' she corrected. But she did relax slightly, aware that this Guy wouldn't harm her.

''Your arm is bruised,'' he said, scowling. ''Why, when I'd do anything in my power to protect you, am I forced to become the one who hurts you?''

His angry distress moved her. If only she was free to comfort him without worrying about what might ensue if they touched. ''It's not you,'' she reminded him. ''Or me, for that matter.''

He shook his head. ''If I hadn't heard that voice in my head asking me what my name was, I might well have dropped you into the bayou.''

She stared at him. ''What voice?''

He shrugged. ''A man's. I didn't understand at first—I think he spoke in French.''

''Could he have been your Revenir ancestor?''

"Once or twice I thought my ancestor might have spoken to me in dreams. But this time?" He shook his head. "Why would he take me over, force me to relive his past, then help me—help us both—by asking me a question that would bring me back to myself?"

Intrigued by the puzzle Guy posed, Lia forgot what she was wearing. Sliding off the bed, she walked to a window and gazed at the lowering sky. Wind bent the tree branches and swirled debris high. Ophelia was on the way. Her storm or the other's?

"We'll have to see it through." Guy spoke from close behind her. "The storm and..." He didn't finish.

What he left unsaid chilled Lia. Evangeline's unsatisfied hunger for revenge still drove her. She'd never stop until Guy Russell, the last of the Revenirs, was hers. And he could be hers only in death. His death.

"You can't have him," Lia whispered. "Never."

"What did you say?" he asked.

She turned to find him nearer than she'd thought. Even if she'd wanted to repeat her words she couldn't have because his lips were so close to hers that nothing else mattered.

They met each other halfway and he wrapped his arms around her as though he'd never let her go. His mouth covered hers in the kiss they both so desperately wanted and needed, a kiss that belonged to them alone.

Deaf to the wind whipping around the house, rattling shutters and plucking loose shingles from the roof, blind to the dark and threatening clouds rolling toward them and oblivious of the menace that could neither be heard nor seen, they clung together in a timeless embrace.

CHAPTER FOURTEEN

Downstairs in the kitchen, the lights were on against the gloom shrouding the late afternoon. Between bursts of static, the radio warned of hurricane-force winds and torrential rain. Sulie, unruffled, removed a pecan pie from the oven and set it on a rack to cool. The lights flickered, then steadied, flickered and steadied again.

"Be candles and matches up there—" she pointed to the corner cupboard "—for when we be needing them. Be hurricane lanterns stored in the pantry."

How can she go on calmly cooking when she knows what's coming? Lia asked herself. When there's not just the storm but the Dread One to worry about.

As if in answer, Sulie said, "No matter what, folks got to eat. I be learning that when I be lots younger 'n you two."

Taking that as a deserved reproof, Lia busied herself helping Sulie prepare the evening meal while Guy brought out the lanterns. Some had batteries but the older ones used kerosene and he made certain all were functioning, filling the bases and trimming wicks. He was testing the last lantern when the electricity failed completely, leaving them in the dark except for the lantern's flame.

"It looks as though we'll dine by candlelight this evening," he said.

Under different circumstances it might have been romantic but Lia was too apprehensive to relax and enjoy the meal. Sulie had made a pot of her special Creole coffee and carried a cup to each of them while they were eating the pecan pie for dessert.

"Ordinarily I never take sugar in my coffee," Guy commented, "but this is so strong I don't know if I could drink it unsweetened."

"Noir comme le diable, fort comme la mort, doux comme l'amour, chaud comme l'enfer," Sulie said. "Black as the devil, strong as death, sweet as love, hot as hell, that be Creole coffee."

"You've covered all the bases and home plate as well," Guy admitted.

"And maybe more," Sulie said, enigmatic as usual.

"More?" Guy said suspiciously. "You *have* told us all you know about this de la Roche-Revenir business, haven't you?"

"Me, I only know what Ole Miss be telling. I don't hold nothing she say back from you."

"Evangeline did drown in the bayou?" he asked.

Sulie clutched at the neck of her dress as she often did when Evangeline's name was said aloud. "Ole Miss say she drown, she tell me the papers from the old days say she drown."

"But they never recovered her body," Guy said. "Nor found any trace of him or his body."

"That be what Ole Miss say."

Lia had a sudden inspiration. "Maybe he had a change of heart and they ran away together."

Guy raised his eyebrows. "To live happily ever after, you mean?"

About to insist it was a possibility, Lia changed her mind. Those two could never be happy together. Besides, if they had run away, why would they be here haunting the estate?

Lightning lit the room with a greenish glow and thunder rumbled ominously. Rain slashed against the windows.

"Close but not quite on us yet," Guy said, yawning.

"Didn't you sleep after we came in this morning?" Lia asked.

"Off and on. I kept having this frustrating dream where General Lafayette tried to pass on to me a message of great importance. I tried hard to do as he wished but unfortunately I couldn't understand a word he said because he spoke in his native language— French."

"Think," Sulie ordered. "Maybe some of those French words stayed with you?"

Guy shook his head. "Not a one. What difference does it make? Lafayette and the message was only a dream."

She shook her finger in his face. "Next time you pay attention, you hear? Don't make no never mind you don't be knowing French. You listen and keep the words in your head."

Guy smiled, obviously humoring her. "I hear and I obey."

"See you don't forget." Sulie rose and began carrying dishes from the table to the sink. When Guy started to help, she stopped him. "While me and Miss Lia be redding up the kitchen you can be getting that chest from the secret place in the library."

"I'll be glad to," he said, "but what do you want with the chest?"

"The brooch."

Lia stared at Sulie, wanting to protest but holding her tongue. She'd hoped never to look at the thing again but Sulie wouldn't have asked for the brooch if it wasn't necessary to have it on hand tonight. "Please do as Sulie asks," she said to Guy.

He shrugged and left the kitchen.

"While he be getting the chest and all," Sulie told her, "you quick run up the back stairs, go to the attic and fetch the white gown. We be needing that gown tonight—hide it under your bed."

Although she hated the thought of handling the gown again, Lia didn't argue. Choosing one of the battery lanterns, she obeyed. As she climbed the attic steps, she heard not only the pounding of the rain on the roof but the telltale plinking that warned of leaks. Reaching the attic, she held the lantern high to look for water coming in but merely succeeded in making the shadows shift eerily, as though hidden watchers stalked her.

Assuring herself there was nothing to be afraid of, she crossed to the wardrobe, removed the white gown and hurried from the attic. In her room, she thrust the gown under the bed, shuddering at the idea of possibly having to wear it and hoping Sulie wouldn't ask her to. She reentered the kitchen as Guy came in from the library carrying the box containing the brooch.

He offered it to her but she shrank back and so he handed the box to Sulie, who took out the brooch, put it in her apron pocket and continued washing the dishes.

"No explanation?" Annoyance tinged Guy's voice.

"Me, I need to be keeping this for a while," Sulie said without so much as a glance at him.

Guy shrugged, raising his eyebrows at Lia, then stifled another yawn.

"If you're sleepy," she said, "why fight it? Go up to bed."

He shook his head. "We have to stay together tonight. The storm—"

"This house," Sulie said, turning from the sink to face him, "it last through storm after storm for over a hundred years. It gonna last through this."

"The house be damned," he growled. "I'm worried about Lia and me lasting through the bloody storm. You told us Evangeline drowned in a storm. So maybe he's waiting until tonight. Maybe that's why he didn't shove her in the bayou when he had the chance. I mean when I had the chance." He rubbed his hand over his forehead. "Oh, hell, I'm so tired I can't think straight."

Sulie touched Lia's shoulder. "You go upstairs with him, stay with him."

"But—"

Sulie's dark eyes held hers. "Me, I don't be telling you wrong. You got to trust me."

Lia wasn't certain she could trust anyone, not even herself, but she realized Guy, who was falling asleep on his feet, wouldn't go to his room without her. Considering how exhausted he was, the other wasn't likely to take him over. It should be safe enough for her to stay with him until he fell asleep.

"Okay," she said to him, "together it is."

In his room, Guy kicked off his moccasins, pulled off his T-shirt and dropped onto his bed still dressed in his jeans. "Don't leave me," he mumbled as his eyes closed. "Stay here."

Lia looked down at him, marveling at how quickly he'd fallen asleep. Leaning toward him, she gently brushed a stray strand of auburn hair from his forehead. How peaceful he looked, almost like the young boy he'd once been.

She sighed, remembering that his boyhood couldn't have been all that peaceful considering how long he'd been plagued by dreams of the woman in white. Leaning closer, she touched her lips briefly to his. Though the kiss didn't rouse him, he smiled and she hoped she'd brought him a pleasant dream for a change.

Straightening, her attention was caught by the furry gris-gris wrapped around the bedpost she stood next to. One beady brown eye stared at her and she grimaced, belatedly realizing the eye was made of glass.

"Protect him," she whispered to the thing, at the same time knowing in her heart that no amulet could save him from the Dread One. Could anything or anyone?

A lump came into her throat as she tried to imagine life without Guy. "I love you," she whispered, struggling against the impulse to fling herself onto the bed beside him and hold him in her arms.

She forced herself to turn away from the bed, aware that her presence in his room couldn't stop the Dread One. She could try to save him only through her power, if she understood how to use it properly. She knew she had more to learn. Would she master what she needed in time? Leaving the still-lit battery lantern on the dresser where he'd set it, Lia stepped into the hall.

Sulie was waiting for her with a kerosene lantern, the white gown from the attic folded over her arm. She motioned for Lia to follow her, leading the way to the room near the main staircase, the room with no furnishings, the locked room that supposedly had no key. Removing an old-fashioned brass key from her apron pocket, Sulie handed it to Lia.

Certain this had been Evangeline's room, Lia swallowed twice before inserting the key into the lock. Though she'd peered through the keyhole when she'd first come to the house and had seen nothing but an empty room, still she turned the key with trepidation. Taking a deep breath, she eased the door open.

Sulie nudged her from behind, urging her to step inside. Holding herself tensely, Lia crossed the threshold and looked quickly around, grimacing against the smell of mold and mildew. By the dim light of Sulie's lantern, she saw no furnishings except for a cheval mirror tucked into one corner. The room, which obviously had never been remodeled or refinished like the other rooms in the mansion, had no closet.

The windows, bare of draperies, were festooned with cobwebs, the panes clouded with dirt. Dust dulled the polish of the hardwood floor.

"No one ever come in here for years and years." Sulie spoke in a whisper. She nodded toward the mirror. "You got to be watching yourself put this gown on, I be telling you what to say."

Lia fought to control her revulsion at the thought of wearing the gown Sulie thrust at her. Holding it reluctantly, she muttered, "This was *hers.*"

"Why else you think you got to wear it?"

"I don't want to—to change again. To be her."

"Be a ward-off spell to stop that." As she spoke, a vicious onslaught of wind-driven rain slammed against the windows, rattling them. Sulie set the lantern on the floor, glancing uneasily over her shoulder. "Hurry!"

Facing the mirror, seeing only bits and pieces of herself because the silvered back was badly worn, Lia stripped. She would have left on her bra and briefs but Sulie shook her head, wordlessly telling her she was to wear nothing but the gown.

Sulie offered her an old hairbrush whose silver handle was tarnished black. Not wanting to touch it but realizing this must be part of some ritual, Lia forced herself to brush her hair with the ancient relic until it became a dark cloud above the white of the gown.

"You listen, say what I say," Sulie ordered, holding the brooch on her right palm like an offering. The gleam of the emerald in the flickering lantern light caught Lia's attention as she obeyed.

When Sulie finished, she nodded to Lia. Her gaze still fixed on the emerald, Lia intoned:

"As I am, I remain
In the light.
No dark can touch me
In the light.
What is dark
I turn to light.
Light overcomes darkness
I am the light."

Sulie nodded and knelt beside the lantern, gesturing for Lia to join her. When Lia dropped to her knees, Sulie turned the brooch over and opened the back compartment.

"Burn his hair." She spoke so low Lia barely heard her.

Lia wondered if this could have been the reason the brooch had appeared in her room that time. So she'd burn the hair. In that case, maybe Evangeline hadn't been responsible for putting the brooch there. Maybe Ole Miss had done it. But for what reason Lia didn't know. She had no idea why the hair must be burned. But now wasn't the time to question Sulie.

Plucking the auburn strands gingerly from the brooch, Lia eased open the top of the lantern and dropped the hair into the flame where it writhed and twisted as though trying to escape the fire. A dreadful stink filled the room. Lightning flashed, a deafening thunderclap shook the house. Something crashed against a window, a pane broke and a broken branch from the magnolia by the gazebo thrust into the room, scattering broken glass over the floor.

With shaking hands, Sulie pinned the now-empty brooch below the neckline of the white gown Lia wore, then scrambled to her feet. With Lia following, they hurried from the room, relocking it but leaving the key in the door.

Lia was certain the noise had roused Guy but when she glanced in on him he was still asleep. Sulie grasped her hand, leading her along the hall to the back stairs. In the kitchen Sulie set the lantern on the table.

"He don't wake," she told Lia. "Me, I put a sleeping potion in his coffee."

Still shaken by what had happened in the room upstairs, for a moment or two Lia couldn't speak. "Why?" she asked when she could get the word out.

"So he be sleeping so deep she can't be luring him from his bed. 'Sides, he ain't never gonna let you wear that gown if he knows. That brooch, neither. He don't understand power."

"I'm not so sure I understand power myself," Lia confessed.

Sulie gave her an appraising look. "Maybe it help if you use Kos. His power be inside you now. When evil threatens, you got to find Kos in yourself and throw him at the darkness. You got to always remember light be stronger than dark."

"You know so much more than I do," Lia said. "I should think you could fight her far better than I."

Sulie shook her head. "Me, I know things but my power be weak. Gris-gris, yes, I make gris-gris. Stand up to the Dread One, that be beyond my power. She squish me like she squish a cricket, real easy. 'Sides, I ain't no de la Roche. It take one of her blood to stand against her."

This made as much sense to Lia as anything else did. She sat at the table in the white gown Evangeline had once worn and thought over what she learned about her dangerous adversary of an ancestor.

"If she hadn't drowned before her baby was born," Lia said, "the child would have been both de la Roche and Revenir."

Sulie merely grunted but Lia couldn't dismiss the child who'd never been born. What if, because of the wild—and unprotected—couplings she and Guy had been forced into, she was pregnant? She could never feel the baby was really hers and Guy's, she would always think of it as belonging to the others.

Recalling the horrible malformations of Maurice's unborn baby that Evangeline had put into her mind, Lia shuddered. What if she did happen to be pregnant and Evangeline did that to the baby she carried?

"No!" she cried and buried her face in her hands.

She felt a hand on her shoulder. "You gonna give up?" Sulie demanded. "Let her be taking your man to his death?"

Slowly, dispiritedly, Lia raised her head. How could anyone prevail against Evangeline's malevolence?

"She be doing this to you," Sulie warned her. "Can't take you over no more, so she be trying to make you feel weak, make you feel you can't stand up to her."

Lia blinked. Was Sulie telling her the truth? If so, she refused to be intimidated. She had no one to call on for help, no one to depend on except herself. But, no matter how impossible the odds seemed to her she couldn't, she wouldn't, give up without a fight.

Rising from the chair, she crossed to the window and stared through its rain-streaked pane into the wild night. *I know you're out there, Evangeline,* she challenged silently, *riding the storm in a way I can't. I know you're bent on vengeance and I know you have dark and terrible powers. But I am Ophelia and this is my storm. I oppose you. I will never let you take what rightfully belongs to me.*

CHAPTER FIFTEEN

With mounting apprehension, Guy noticed the white mist gathering above him. He dreaded what would happen next but he was powerless to prevent it. The mist thickened, then thinned and thickened again. Why was she taking so long to come to him?

Was she deliberately prolonging his agony?

A beady brown eye stared glassily through the mist which was thinning once more, seemingly on the verge of dissipating. The eye had never appeared before— what was it a part of? A word that he couldn't quite grasp hung on the edge of his mind. Though he couldn't reach the word, he had a vague idea that the eye was protecting him in some strange way.

Nothing had ever protected him before and he feared it wouldn't last. A word echoed in his head. *Remember. Remember.* But what was he supposed to remember? He didn't know.

The mist began to thicken again, hiding the eye, forming into the shape of a woman. She hovered over him, misty white. *"Je reviens,"* she whispered, smiling triumphantly at her victory over the eye.

She'd returned not only to him but for him. She beckoned in the gesture that meant he must follow where she led, follow her whether he wished to or not.

Unable to resist, he tried, as always, to do as she bade him. To his surprise, he found himself unable to move a muscle.

His legs, his arms, his body refused to obey his command to rise and follow. It was as though invisible chains held him in place. For a time she watched his struggle with a dark, unfathomable gaze. He couldn't believe his eyes when she began to dissolve and he stared at the spot where she'd been even after she'd completely vanished.

Gone. She was gone. But gone was not necessarily vanquished. He knew she'd return. And he could do nothing to prevent her return. All he could do was wait.

Suddenly he seemed to be gazing down into black water—the bayou. Yet he knew he hadn't moved, he knew intangible chains still held him. Neither she nor anyone else was in sight but he heard a voice, a man's voice.

"Ray ven aze O!" the voice commanded. *"Ray ven aze e c!"* It repeated the meaningless syllables once more and then fell silent. The words circled in Guy's mind. French, he thought. He didn't understand French. What had the man said to him? Had it been the same voice he'd heard twice before? That voice had spoken in English as well as French. If it was the same man, why hadn't he translated?

The bayou vanished, he was somewhere else, lying in darkness, still chained.

"Je reviens." This time her whisper preceded her, warning of her return. The darkness gradually light-

ened and his heart filled with despair when he saw her floating toward him in her flowing white gown. She paused and beckoned to him.

Compelled by her to follow, he strained to rise. For a moment he could not and then he began to move but not as he usually did. Something was different. He was different. He felt reduced in size, insubstantial, as though he'd been condensed and imprisoned like a genie in a bottle and then someone had pulled the cork, enabling him to ease through the small opening. He felt himself expand as he emerged but he knew he was still different.

Looking around, he found he wasn't on the gray plain but in a room. His bedroom at the mansion, he realized when he saw Lafayette's picture on the wall. Someone was sprawled on the bed. Who?

Guy stared in fearful wonder. The body lying on the bed was his. He understood then that he was floating free of his body, that she'd pulled him from his body to drift through the air as she was drifting.

He followed her from his room, along the hall and down the stairs, helpless to resist, even though he was well aware she led him to his doom. The Dread One floated into the kitchen where Sulie sat at the table. The old woman shivered, glanced all around and hugged herself but he knew she couldn't see either of them.

Lia stood in a white gown at the window gazing into the night. The wraith approached her, smiling mockingly. When Lia whirled, staring, he felt a flicker of hope but it died almost immediately. Though Lia had obviously felt the Dread One's presence, she couldn't see her, either. Or see him.

The wraith floated through the closed door. To his horror he was sucked along in her wake. In desperation he called soundlessly to Lia but she didn't seem to hear. The last he saw as he left the kitchen was her hand rising to clutch at the emerald brooch.

Outside, though he was aware of the gusting wind and lashing rain, he couldn't actually feel either. The Dread One drifted through the storm, her destination, he knew, the bayou.

Lia shook her head quickly back and forth to rid herself of what she was certain had been an hallucination. She couldn't actually have seen Guy vanishing through the closed door of the kitchen into the storm. Impossible.

And yet something had raised the hair on her nape, convincing her that evil hovered nearby. "Sulie—" she began.

"She pass by here," the old woman said. "Me, I feel her."

"I know it's unbelievable," Lia said, "but I thought I saw Guy pass through a closed door just now."

Sulie leapt from her chair, ran across the kitchen and shoved Lia toward the back door. "Go after him. You be seeing his spirit, not him. She can't rouse him 'cause of my sleeping potion so she force his spirit to leave his body. Stop her! Tell his spirit to return to his body or he gonna die."

Terrified by Sulie's words, Lia flung the door open and dashed into the night. Buffeted by the wind, she ducked her head to keep the rain from blinding her completely. She tried to set a course for the bayou but the wind was too strong to combat. She could never reach Guy in time. Not physically. She'd have to try another way.

Huddling in the meager shelter of a thick growth of oleanders, she closed her eyes and summoned her power. She felt the thrum as it rose, enclosing her in a place apart. She searched for Guy, calling his name silently but she couldn't find the slightest trace of him.

Refusing to give way to despair, she finally remembered that she'd been gripping the emerald brooch when she saw his spirit. She immediately closed her hand over the brooch and called again.

This time his face formed in her mind. *Come to me,* she urged silently. *Come because I call you. Because I love you, you are bound to me. You must not follow her, you must come to me. Now.* Over and over she sent her silent call. The words felt right, she prayed that they were. Truth was in the words—she loved him, she would love him forever.

She sensed his approach before she saw him drifting slowly toward her through the wind-driven rain. In her relief, she almost ran to embrace him but then she noticed he was neither rain drenched nor windblown. A spirit, as Sulie had told her. Swallowing her awe, she took a deep breath and gave him a silent order.

Return to the house, to your room, to your bed, to your body. Do not leave your body again. You must

*do as I say and only as I say. Because I love you, you
are bound to me.*

He drifted past her toward the house, unaffected by
the storm, and she watched him until the rain hid him
from her sight, increasingly aware of the malevolence
flowing toward her from the bayou, knowing she and
her love for him was all that stood between his spirit
and the Dread One.

Between one breath and the next, evil surrounded
her, probing for weakness, seeking to enter, to pos-
sess her. Unsure of how to protect herself, Lia struggled to fend off the attack, acutely aware that if
Evangeline took her over, both she and Guy were
doomed.

Images wormed their way into her mind, more horrible than the malformed unborn baby Evangeline had
once threatened her with, ghastly pictures of a dis-
eased Guy, of herself rotting inside and out. When at
last Lia found a way to close her mind's eye to the evil
images, the attack changed direction.

Suddenly Lia couldn't breathe. As she gasped for
air, her heart slowed beat by beat, on the verge of
stopping altogether. Her knees buckled, she was falling, losing consciousness. "Kos!" she cried frantically.

He was there, coiled in her mind. In desperation she
summoned her failing strength to fling her image of
the snake at the Dread One. Air rushed into her lungs
and her heart began to beat in a normal rhythm. The
Dread One's grip on her senses eased until she was
again aware of the rain and the wind lashing her.

Had she won?

Triumphant laughter filled her mind, warning Lia the battle was far from over. She tensed, seeing something or someone approaching, a dark figure slogging through the storm toward her, as rain drenched as she was. Guy! In the flesh, body and spirit united.

"Guy!" she cried, running toward him. He brushed past her as though she didn't exist and her heart sank. Once again he'd been summoned by the Dread One and was helplessly following where she led.

Her silent call had reached his spirit but, without even trying, Lia knew she couldn't reach him now that he was flesh and blood. Fighting the wind, she plodded grimly after him, determined not to give up. The white wraith floating ahead of Guy gave off an eerie green glow, undimmed by the storm, enabling Lia to keep him in sight.

In her struggle against the wind and rain, Lia felt as though she were caught in a nightmare where the dreamer, no matter how frantically she tries, can't force her legs to run. On and on she slogged, never quite able to catch up to Guy. And then, though she couldn't see it, she knew the bayou lay dead ahead. The white wraith halted and reached toward him.

Once she touched him, he'd be lost forever.

"Guy!" Lia screamed.

Though he hadn't seemed to hear her cry out to him before, he hesitated, half turning. In a burst of speed born of her desperation, Lia flung herself between him and the Dread One, wrapping her arms around Guy so that, if he walked on, she was between him and the evil that lured him to destruction.

A savage gust of wind sent them both staggering, forcing them back, away from the bayou, the storm thrusting them away from Evangeline, as well. Guy didn't struggle when Lia grabbed his hand, pulling him with her as she let the wind drive them where it would, understanding that it was her storm to use, after all. Evangeline's spell was broken—but for how long?

Guy, though still dazed from the trance as well as battered by the storm, was aware enough to realize that by some miracle he'd escaped from the Dread One. Holding tightly to Lia, he fled with the wind, unsure where they were headed but knowing it was away from the bayou. Whether they could escape Evangeline or not was another matter. He damn well meant to do his best.

On and on they stumbled until it seemed they'd been within the storm's grip forever. When at last Guy connected with something solid he had no idea what it was or where they were until his groping fingers felt the polished surface of the marble crypt. Reasoning they couldn't go on much longer, he pulled Lia around with him to take shelter on the lee side of the stone where there was some respite from the wind.

"Rest here for a bit." He pitched his voice to carry over the shriek of the wind. When she collapsed to lie limply against him, he wondered if she'd be able to go on at all.

He put his mouth to her ear. "Lia? Are you okay?"

"Tired," she murmured. Because of the storm's noise he barely heard her.

Relieved she was conscious, he huddled close to the stone, cradling her in his arms as he gently pushed her sodden hair back from her face, then held her close, shielding her as best he could from the wind and rain. "My love, my love," he whispered, aware she wouldn't be able to hear his words but needing to say them.

She'd risked her life to save him and she'd won, but he feared the victory was only temporary. The Dread One still prowled through the storm and she'd find them sooner or later. Should they try to reach the house? He shook his head. Though they'd be out of the storm, she could find them there as easily as here. Besides, even if he was able to locate the house when he couldn't see more than a foot in front of him, he doubted if Lia had enough strength left to make it that far.

Though the marble crypt did help to cut the wind, it did nothing to stop the deluge of rain. He'd never been so wet in his life. The very ground underneath him was awash. It occurred to him that he might try to open the crypt—after all, it was empty—and bring Lia inside with him, but the idea filled him with revulsion. Evangeline might never have been buried here but it was her grave all the same.

Remembering that a hurricane had an eye, a temporary calm before the second half of the storm hit, he decided that when the eye passed over them, he'd make a run for the house, carrying Lia if he had to. If they must wait for doom to fall they might as well be more comfortable.

Lia stirred in his arms and he realized she was saying something he couldn't hear. He bent so she could speak in his ear.

"Where is she?" Lia asked.

He shook his head.

"She won't give up," Lia warned.

"I know."

"I'm so tired. What if I can't call up my power?"

His arms tightened around her. "She doesn't want you, she wants me. You're in danger only if you try to stand in her way. Don't risk yourself. Stay alive. Promise me, Lia."

"We'll both live," she said with sudden fierceness. "Or we'll die together."

As her words settled into his heart he covered her lips with his, meaning the kiss as a promise of life even while he feared for them both.

She didn't respond to his kiss. He drew back, alarmed, realizing belatedly she'd gone limp again. "Are you all right?" he asked.

She didn't answer.

"Lia," he pleaded, "speak to me."

When she didn't reply, he shifted her in his arms, trying to make sure she was still breathing. Her head lolled to one side.

"Lia!" he shouted, frantic.

No matter what he tried, she remained totally unresponsive. He was about to hoist her over his shoulder and make a desperate attempt to find the house when he felt her stir in his arms.

Before he could say or do anything, she pushed away from him and sprang to her feet. He stared up at her uncomprehendingly. She smiled down at him, a mockingly cruel smile.

"Je reviens," she whispered.

Guy leapt up. Lia's face, her entire body glowed with an eerie green light. It was not like before, when Evangeline had taken over Lia. This time she was not merely Evangeline, lusting for her lover, she was also the Dread One and she possessed Lia.

In another moment she'd beckon him and he'd be helpless, following her to the bayou, following Lia to the bayou....

And then he understood the full extent of Evangeline's revenge. Lia wasn't safe, she'd never been safe. It wouldn't simply be the Dread One luring him into the bayou to drown, Lia would drown, too, because the Dread One wore Lia's body. Under the Dread One's spell, he'd be forced to watch Lia go to her death before he died.

And there was nothing he could do to prevent it.

Remember! The man's cry reverberated in his head.

What? What? he thought frantically. What must I remember?

"Je reviens," Lia whispered for the second time.

The French words triggered his memory. As her hand rose to beckon him, he sought desperately to pull from his mind what were to him nonsense syllables.

"Ray ven aze O!" he shouted at the Dread One. *"Ray ven aze e c!"*

For a long, breath-held moment nothing happened. Then the green glow outlining Lia began to fade and, at the same time, water swirled around and over Guy's ankles. His attention on Lia, he hardly noticed the water rising until a strong current nearly swept him off his feet. Lia staggered, falling, and, with a desperate lunge, he caught her.

Boosting her to the top of the crypt, he pulled himself up to join her. Dazed, she clung to him as the water rose higher and higher. Floodwater from the bayou, he told himself, holding her close to him, trying not to believe that the Dread One, frustrated in her efforts to lure him to the bayou, instead had brought the bayou to him.

In his concern over the rising water, he didn't at first note the change in the wind as it began to die down. Only when the rain eased did he realize the storm was letting up.

The eye, he thought. It offered a chance to reach the house. Unfortunately, they were trapped here by the water.

"She's gone," Lia said. "It's over." As if evoked by her words, the moon slid into sight from behind thinning clouds.

Silver light gleamed on the water surrounding the crypt. As they watched, the dark water began to swirl round and round the stone, the level dropping rapidly until only puddles remained.

He slid from the top and helped Lia down. "Are you up to making a run for the house?" he asked.

She didn't answer, she wasn't even looking at him. Frowning, he followed her gaze. The bronze doors to the vault stood open, the chain dangling from one of the handles. Lia slipped her hand into his as, step by slow step they approached the open doors, the soggy ground catching at their feet as though trying to prevent their passage.

When they reached the open doors and bent to peer inside, Lia gasped. "Something's in there!"

Something ivory white, he saw. Inching closer, he realized he was looking at bones littering the floor of the vault. A skeleton. Beside him, Lia unfastened the emerald brooch from the white gown she wore and flung it into the vault. He started when the bronze doors began to move. With a clang they swung shut.

Guy and Lia stared at one another. "The bayou brought her bones back," Lia whispered.

He strode to the doors, took one end of the rusty chain, threaded it through the other handle, affixed the old padlock through the links and snapped it shut with a final click.

The click echoed in his mind for as long as it took them—it seemed forever—to make their weary trek to the house. Had they really seen the last of the Dread One?

Later, dry and dressed in clean clothes, Lia and Guy sat with Sulie at the kitchen table drinking coffee and finishing off the pecan pie by lantern light as they waited out the other half of the storm. Sulie had already been told the entire story.

"Say them words again," Sulie asked Guy. "They be French but you don't be easy to understand."

"Ray ven aze O," he said. *"Ray ven aze e c."*
Sulie nodded. "*'Revenez os. Revenez ici.'* That be what he tell you to remember. Means, return bones. Return here.'"

Guy glanced at Lia, who was gazing raptly at him. "Your ancestor," she said. "The other Guy, the Revenir. He came to your rescue. To our rescue."

"Must be a Revenir got to say the words of the spell to the Dread One," Sulie put in, "and the words, they got to be said in French 'cause she don't never learn English." She shook her head at Guy. "You may be a lawyer but you sure don't be quick to learn. Good thing you finally caught on—be almost too late."

Guy smiled tiredly. "Better late than never."

"Anyway, she be at rest now," Sulie said. "The Dread One don't be haunting this place no more."

By the time he and Lia dragged up the stairs to bed, the storm had lessened to the point where Sulie was predicting sunshine by morning.

Though neither of them had discussed sleeping arrangements, he took Lia's hand when they reached their bedroom doors and led her into his room. "I was going to come in, invited or not," she admitted.

Once they were in bed, he drew her into his arms— and fell asleep.

Guy found himself standing by the bayou in what was neither day nor night but what he instinctively understood was a perpetual twilight. The dark waters flowed past, still mysterious, though no longer sinister in his eyes.

He felt rather than saw a figure forming beside him and stiffened, fearing to look, waiting in dread for the terrible whisper.

I didn't kill her. The man's voice spoke in his mind.

Guy glanced to his left at the vague and insubstantial form of a man. He couldn't make out his features.

We quarreled on the bayou bank, as you know, the voice continued. *She slipped, I tried to save her but I failed. My guilt is that I didn't jump in and make an attempt to rescue her, my excuse is that I could no more swim than she could.*

"What did you do then?" Guy asked when the voice said no more.

What could I do? I loved her. I failed her. There was nothing left for me. I walked back to the de la Roche estate after riding home, entered the garçonnière and wandered from one painting to the next. By the time I reached the last, overwhelmed by the knowledge I could never hold her in my arms again, I slashed the canvas with my hunting knife, laid myself on the chaise longue where we'd so often made love and cut my throat.

"But why was this never brought out? Who found you?"

Her father, of course. He and my father had been enemies from the day my mother chose to wed a Revenir instead of a de la Roche. Because he hated me,

*her father dug my grave in secret, in the dark, in the
storm. He buried me and never told a soul.*

"Where is your grave?" Guy asked.

*I'm surprised you haven't worked that out for
yourself. Perhaps the Revenir blood is thinning. He
buried me where Evangeline's grave is now. He had the
crypt erected there to prevent my body from ever rising to the surface, as bodies tend to do in these Louisiana lowlands.*

*I do not say "au revoir" to you, not because you
aren't a speaker of French but because we will not
meet again. I will never return. Nor will Evangeline.
She is at peace at last, after these many years. Thus I,
too, may rest. So in parting I use English words, I say,
Fare-thee-well. May you and your love fare well and
find the happiness denied to Evangeline and to me.*

Despite all the torment this unquiet spirit had put
him through, in the end, Guy admitted, he'd re-
deemed himself.

"Farewell," Guy murmured.

"You're talking in your sleep," a voice accused.

Guy opened his eyes. In the faint light coming
through the windows, he saw Lia lying next to him in
his bed.

"I was saying goodbye to my ancestor's spirit," he
told her.

Her eyes widened and she started to sit up. Guy
reached for her, pulling her into his arms. "Like
Evangeline, the other Guy is gone for good," he murmured. "They're both at rest."

She fit into his arms perfectly, as if meant to be there. As far as he was concerned, she *was* meant to be there. He had no intention of letting her go and was about to tell her so when she spoke.

"Was it a good dream?" she asked.

"I wouldn't call it a dream, not exactly."

"Did he talk to you? What did he say?"

Guy told her, ending with, "His final wish was for me and my love to know the happiness he and Evangeline never found."

When she didn't comment, he pulled her closer and kissed her, careful to make his embrace tentative, fearing Lia might be reminded of what they'd been forced to do by the others. Her eager response reassured him and he deepened the kiss, his hand caressing the enticing curve of her hip.

After a moment she pulled away a little and murmured, "If we're going to make love, you've got to do something about that gris-gris on the bedpost because I won't have him watching us with that beady little eye of his."

Guy solved the problem by stripping off his pajama bottoms and hanging them over the post and the gris-gris. When he slid down in the bed again, Lia welcomed him into her arms. To his delight, like him, she now wore nothing.

"This is us, just the two of us," he said softly.

"Umm," she agreed, winding her arms around his neck. Though he'd intended to go slow and easy, she kissed him with such fiery passion that he forgot what he'd meant to do, forgot that and everything else as he immersed himself in the joy of shared desires.

Their lovemaking culminated in a wild, triumphant joining that united them, body and spirit.

Later, snuggled in his arms, she murmured, "You said your ancestor wished happiness for you and your love but you haven't yet told me who your love is."

He smiled to himself. "I've been thinking it over," he said.

"And?"

"I'm close to a decision," he said, his hand cupping her breast. "If you wouldn't mind a repeat of what we did a while ago, I'll let you know immediately afterward."

"Maybe I will and maybe I won't."

He raised up on his elbow and looked down at her. "What do you mean, maybe you won't?"

"How do I know what your next request will be? If you promise never to ask me to do any private dances for you, I might agree to the repeat."

The teasing note in her voice warmed him. If she could joke about what they'd been through, everything would be all right. "No private dances," he said. "Unless, of course, you decide on your own to—"

She put her fingers over his mouth and said, "I won't agree unless you tell me beforehand who your love is."

He cupped her face in his hands. "From the moment we met in Oakland, I knew in my heart there'd never be anyone else for me but you, no other love but you."

CHAPTER SIXTEEN

In the car, on the way to DuBois, LaBranche and Charters, Lia hugged to herself the knowledge that she no longer need worry about carrying a child that she might never be able to feel was hers and Guy's. She definitely wasn't pregnant. She would tell him eventually but not now.

"You're sure this is what you want to do?" Guy asked as he parked near the law offices.

"I'm positive. Nothing can make me change my mind."

He nodded.

When they reached Mr. DuBois's door, the lawyer himself opened it and ushered them in. He shook hands with Guy and bent over hers. When they were seated he walked around to the other side of his desk and sat down.

"I wish we'd had the chance to discuss some of this before my trip to Europe," he said.

Lia said nothing, though she remembered very well how she'd tried without result to get him to open up during that first meeting.

Looking at Guy, DuBois said, "I do confess I was remiss in not admitting immediately that I called you by the wrong name because you reminded me so much of Tanguay Revenir, who'd been a client of mine. I knew, of course, that Tanguay had died without legitimate issue and so I decided it was best not to say anything."

Lia couldn't let that one go by. "Even though you knew the Revenirs and the de la Roches had been enemies in the past?" she asked.

DuBois spread his hands. "So long ago! And so much of it hearsay by the time the tales passed through the generations."

Guy cleared his throat. "Ms. de la Roche is here about her inheritance," he reminded both of them.

"Yes, I understand." DuBois focused on Lia. "As I told your counselor, I've determined that the storm damage to the mansion renders it uninhabitable until extensive repairs are made. Therefore, since an act of God made it impossible for you to fulfill the three-month residence requirement, it is automatically set aside."

"Guy's told me all that," Lia said. "I want to sell the property as soon as possible."

DuBois nodded. "As soon as the will is probated, I'll arrange for the estate to be listed with local realtors." He glanced from her to Guy and back. "Your counselor states you don't intend to keep what monies are due after the property is sold. Is that true?"

"It is." Even now she shuddered inwardly at accepting anything that came from the de la Roches.

After the storm she'd wanted to refuse the legacy entirely but had changed her mind when Guy pointed out that most likely Rebecca would inherit. Rebecca not only didn't need the money, but, as Guy said, didn't deserve any of it, being at least partly responsible for Lia's involvement.

"As I'm sure Mr. Russell advised you," DuBois said to her, "if that is your intent, then it would be wise to deed the estate, after probate but before the sale, to the two I'm told you mean to divide the money between—specifically Maurice Roche and Sulie Mason. Otherwise, you'd be responsible for taxes accruing from that money."

"Whatever's best," she said, "I'd appreciate it if you could arrange all the details."

"Quite naturally you're eager to return to California," DuBois said. "I'll be happy to act as your agent in this matter. I regret that your stay in Louisiana has not been happier."

As they left the office, his last words remained with Lia. Though he'd spoken the truth, the greatest happiness of her life had arisen like a phoenix from the ashes of the terror and despair she'd experienced at the mansion.

"I can't blame you for doing it," Guy said once they reached the car, "but you're giving away a sizable fortune to Maurice and Sulie."

"I know Sulie seems content enough living with Maurice and Dee and she's looking forward to the baby being born as much as they are. But she's worked for the de la Roches most of her life, while Maurice has been snubbed by them for all of his. They deserve that money and I don't want any part of it."

She looked up into his golden eyes and smiled, her heart speeding as she saw his gaze soften with love. "After all," she murmured as his arms closed around her, "didn't I find something in Louisiana far more valuable than any amount of wealth? Didn't I find you?"

*   *   *   *   *

MILLION DOLLAR SWEEPSTAKES (III)

Is the future what it's cracked up to be?

How do you tell your boyfriend he's a bore? Find out this March in...

GETTING AWAY WITH IT: JOJO
by Liz Ireland

Wild, wanna-be actress JoJo Giamatti likes to have a good time, and doesn't see the point of worrying about the future. But lately, all her boyfriend, Peter, cared about was climbing his way up some silly corporate ladder. He had turned into such a bore! Why did he care what the people at the office thought, anyway? But when JoJo found herself kissing Peter's irresistible best friend, she knew she had to do something—fast!

The ups and downs of modern life continue with

GETTING A CLUE: TAMMY
by Wendy Mass (April)

GETTING A GRIP: DIG
by Kathryn Jensen (May)

Get smart. Get into "The Loop!"

Silhouette celebrates motherhood in May with...

Debbie Macomber
Jill Marie Landis
Gina Ferris Wilkins

in

Three Mothers & a Cradle

Join three award-winning authors in this
beautiful collection you'll treasure forever.
The same antique, hand-crafted cradle
connects these three heartwarming romances,
which celebrate the joys and excitement of
motherhood. Makes the perfect gift for yourself
or a loved one!

A special celebration of love,

Only from

Silhouette®

—where passion lives.